Tip Tap Flat

Tip Tap Flat

A View of Glasgow

FREIGHT
BOOKS

First published in the UK June 2012
By Freight Books
49–53 Virginia Street
Glasgow G1 1TS
freightbooks.co.uk

A CIP catalogue reference for this book is available from the British Library

ISBN 9781908754066

Typeset by Freight in Adobe Caslon

Printed in the Czech Republic

University of Glasgow THE GLASGOW SCHOOL OF ART

Writings on Glasgow
from Glasgow School of Art and the University of Glasgow

Editors
Henry Bell
Defne Cizakca
Geneva Sills
Louise Welsh

Thanks to
Stefanie Lehmann for her organisational skills, good humour and sharp eyes and for acting as first copy editor. Gillebrìde MacMillan for help with selections of submissions in Gaelic and translations from Gaelic into English. Glasgow School of Art and the University of Glasgow for funding this anthology and for their contributions towards funding the post of writer in residence. Creative Scotland for their contribution towards funding the post of writer in residence.

Henry Bell was born in Bristol in 1989 and moved to Glasgow in 2008. He is studying for an undergraduate MA in Theology and Literature at the University of Glasgow. As well as writing prose and poetry, Henry founded and helps run Saor Phalastain, an organisation promoting Cultural Resistance and Exchange in Scotland and Palestine.

Defne Cizakca was born in Cyprus, grew up in Turkey and has lived in Malaysia, Germany, Belgium, the Netherlands, Morocco and now Scotland. She is currently completing a creative writing PhD at the university of Glasgow. Her novel is a magically real account of 19th century Istanbul.

Stefanie Lehmann was born in São Paulo in 1991 and has lived in Brazil, Germany, and Canada. She moved to Glasgow in 2010 to undertake undergraduate studies in English Literature at the University of Glasgow.

Gillebrìde MacMillan is a native Gaelic speaker from South Uist in the Western Isles. He works as a Native Language Assistant in Celtic and Gaelic at the University of Glasgow. He is also an internationally acclaimed Gaelic singer and a published writer.

Geneva Sills was born in Chicago in 1987 to father Casey Sills and mother Anne Sills. She earned her BA from Colorado College and is currently pursuing her MFA at the Glasgow School of Art.

Louise Welsh is writer in residence at the University of Glasgow and Glasgow School of Art. She is the author of five novels, several stage plays, short stories and articles; she has also written libretti for opera. Louise has been the recipient of several awards and fellowships, most recently an honorary fellowship from the University of Iowa's International Writing Program. louisewelsh.com

An Introduction from the Editors

'City of the stare', 'Unthank', 'No Mean City', 'Dear Green Place'; Glasgow is Scotland. Glasgow is an overdeveloped aberration, a stain on a rural nation. Glasgow, city of style, city of culture, murder capital, friendliest city in Europe. Glasgow is. Glasgow is. Glasgow is. Glasgow smiles better. A place of hard knocks and John Knox, of love and art and Christ of St John of the Cross. City of tenements, where high-rises crash to the ground. Scarred by motorways, a city founded on rivers where you're rarely far from a park. Red Clydeside and orange walks, Tobacco Lords and slave traders, curry houses and Polish delis. The bird and the bell and the fish and the ring and the tree. It doesn't always rain in Glasgow.

Glasgow; where Robert Wrighim encounters Gilmartin at Finnieston Cross, where young Adam finds love and death on the Forth Clyde Canal, where philosophers resort to a squerr go in Brechin's Bar, where lovers meet between Hope and Union Street.

Glasgow School of Art and the University of Glasgow are internationally renowned institutions, which attract staff, students and visitors from across the globe. They both influence and are influenced by the city they are a part of the heart of. Glasgow is the perfect theme for this anthology of creative writing and graphics from staff and students. Some of them were born and brought up here, others are used to different skies, but all of them belong to our city. They see it with their own eyes. I hope you find these flashes of Glasgow through their vision as enjoyable and as dizzying as I did. This is the city you know, the city you recognise, the city you never saw before, the city you love, the city you hate, this is Glasgow.

Let Glasgow flourish!

Louise Welsh, Writer in Residence at Glasgow School of Art and the University of Glasgow

'There is no one way to begin. It's arbitrary. What you want to find is quintessential truth, the essence of a truth. Now, a truth isn't all fact. A truth is more than a simple fact. A truth is a person's life, a way of looking at something, what made a person do that, what made a society do what it does. Memories are always flawed, so it may not be… it's not statistically accurate. But that something, which that person remembers and the fact that it is remembered and others remember it another way… that same phenomenon… that makes it truth and makes it, as far as I'm concerned, part of history.

I look through the window and I think of early Chicago. There's Lake Michigan and it was on these shores that a city grew. I look at the possibilities within this city. If ever an archetypal American city, it's this. I suppose you want to capture, greedy as I am, as much of the history of this city as you possibly can. And yet, how many dimensions can you cover?'

Excerpt from the 1985 BBC documentary of Studs Terkel, treasured Chicagoan author and collector of oral histories.

Geneva Sills

'In Olinda, if you go out with a magnifying glass and hunt carefully, you may find somewhere a point no bigger than the head of a pin which, if you look at it slightly enlarged, reveals within itself the roofs, the antennas, the skylights, the gardens, the pools, the streamers across the streets, the kiosks in the squares, the horse racing track. That point does not remain there: a year later you will find it the size of half a lemon, then as large as a mushroom, then a soup plate. And then it becomes a full-size city, enclosed within the earlier city: a new city that forces its way ahead in the earlier city and presses it toward the outside.

Olinda is certainly not the only city that grows in concentric circles.'

From Invisible Cities by Italo Calvino. (Remembered on the Glasgow subway, the inner circle.)

Defne Cizakca

'The desert was a real character because of the way all these characters' lives rotated around it and how it changed their lives. They were in flux almost all the time because of the place itself. I felt, even at an early age, that places have a spirit. They're like alive. I remember when I used to come from the mountains back to Beirut, I used to enter the house and think that the house knows that I'm back. I just knew that whenever I was late, and my father would be upset with me, that the house would be upset as well. The house wasn't only furniture. I used to feel that it's like a human being.'

From an interview with the Lebanese author Hanan al-Shaykh

Henry Bell

Contents

Blind Spots

Laura Tansley and Micaela Maftei

The street map her dad lent her was bought from a supermarket in the 90s. It marks every Safeway that isn't there anymore. Now there are delicatessens, artisan bakeries, speciality butchers with pig cheeks and monk fish in the window. She doesn't know how to cook Jerusalem artichokes, or what's in tapenade. This is not a return.

She traces the line of the motorway with a long finger and a stubby nail. With a ruler, as the crow flies, it's fourteen-and-three-quarter centimetres from where she is to Glasgow. The sound of the creases as she opens out the side-flaps is enthralling; the sound of her journey is rung out, a journey of long soft moments, from one end of somewhere to another.

She likes subways, the planners pinned to her wall, logical and direct. Prague, Berlin, London. But the subway here has no map, is one big loop, which means she'll make the same mistakes over and over.

Meredith: clean hair, frank face, Fjällräven backpack. A dusky blue one, faded from use and sudden rain on hills. Heavy socks and thin, strong arms. She has a stack of cards in open envelopes on top of her dresser. Blame is a light thing, a thing with little agency. You can wear it, or you can reject it. It is always your own choice. It hasn't got the power to persist, and anyway it's homeless, just rooting around looking for somewhere to stay for the next few days.

The cards increase monthly, sometimes less frequently. She has almost started to rely on them, which is the great danger. Once this happens, she will have to move on, uproot. No postcode on the cards; no return address at all.

Dear Christina,

Happy Easter. We are thinking of you and wishing for your safety and happiness on this holiday. Your father is better now, and continues to hope for word from you. Elaine is certain his leg will be completely back to normal within six months. That is one of the many things we are grateful for this spring, and hope that you too can share this with us. I enclose a little something that I hope you can use wisely. Please reply, Christina; we only want to know that you are safe and happy.

Dear Christina,

I wonder how close to the 17th this will reach you. I still cannot tell how long it usually takes. Please write and tell me. It's very late and I wonder if I will be able to post this tomorrow. Please let me know when this reaches you, Christina, and try to believe that we only want to know how you are, and to give you our love. I enclose a little something that I hope you can use wisely.

Dear Christina,

Happy Christmas. We love you so much, Christina, and we miss you terribly this year. We want so badly just to know you are safe and happy. Please find some way to give us a sign – please let us know you are alright. I enclose a little something that I hope you can use wisely. Please try to think of me and your father during this holiday.

Dear Christina,

Dear Christina,

Dear Christina,

Dear Christina,

Dearest Christina,

Meredith lasted until the eleventh card before using the money – wisely. No return address, no names. Love, your mother. Love, Mum and Dad. Love from your parents. With all our love. The intensity of the individual feeling combined with the total lack of distinguishing information. The cards were always completely heart-wrenching – some kittens playing with ribbon, a pair of gardening shears on a sun-warmed wooden bench. Always purchased from some charity shop. The envelopes from Woolworths.

When her father was here these buildings didn't exist, they were still husks, scabs rusting. Now they're museums, official buildings, to remind us we built something once; a poet's words carved into the face of its exterior, its interior, its floor, so we know where this place has come from. When her father was here he knew how to pronounce the street names, how to add a growl to a place, how to roll an r in a sentence. But Christina's tongue doesn't curl like his, and her teeth get in the way.

Scars are like landmarks; white nicks from stitches and blisters, strengthening and conditioning, testing limits, piercings that have sealed themselves up. The 90s were all about eyebrows, the 00s the frenulum, foot tattoos and first degree burns. This decade is too young to be marked.

To begin with she did as her father told her and left forwarding addresses. But there were always other older men with advice that was more suited to her situation, like where the next best sunset was, which train had the least ticket inspectors, where to sleep without being moved on. Her father knew all this too, but she had never bothered to ask.

A boy with a cow's lick and a nickname and no real name was with her for a while. She liked to untie his bracelets and rest four fingers on the pale patch of revealed wrist. He had a few friends with floors and a high tog sleeping bag. So they slept on porches, on sofa cushions, cleaned where they could, cooked what they could. But she liked the noise, and he liked the quiet. She liked the traffic, the trappings of travelling with too many people, the chatter and movement. Together, alone, without it, she'd ask would he hum for her to put her to sleep. This was too wearying, so he left to keep looking for quiet. He found the taste of it sometimes, followed it, but could never quite keep hold of it.

Christina had a house once, where people could find her. But she changed all her numbers and instead passed along messages which became more garbled and soon failed to reach the intended. There was a weak link in her game of whispers. Someone who changed 2a to 2b, South to Southwark, Sea to Ocean. These places, these people, had no use for postcodes.

She can see the shadows of him here now, her father, in this city. But she hopes, if he knew what was best for him, that he left sooner rather than later too.

Meredith used the money for vegetables first. Earthy, dense ones: parsnip, swede, carrot. A mist in the cold flat as she boiled dinner into submission. This was wise. Slowly, she ate her way upwards, opening the cards with a more eager finger. Delicate sprouts, steamed and tossed with finely chopped garlic. One day she swapped butter for a glass bottle of olive oil. From then it was purple garlic, vibrant broccoli, a fat beefsteak tomato that lasted two days, and then eventually on to a final graduation of avocado, goat's cheese and then grape tomatoes, burst against her palate with a slender finger that she would then draw out of her mouth, sucking the pale green seeds off. She stopped short at paper-thin scrolls of smoked meat, and wine, even if it was on offer. But the regularity of the cards suggested these were temporary limits, maybe the final few steps in a prolonged, ill-advised, incredible seduction. She didn't stop herself at an umbrella from a charity shop one day when she forgot hers at home. And this allowance opened up for her, leading to a pair of red shoes, a thin leather belt, a grey woollen cardigan.

Sometimes, when she walked in the city, she imagined Christina. Maybe Christina was the bus driver who took enough verbal abuse from various passengers that Meredith eventually stopped taking the bus, even when it rained.

Christina was the crossing guard who somehow knew the name of every child who crossed the road each morning, even through scarves and hoods and the sameness of uniforms. But she must be younger. Perhaps Christina was the one who stamped out library books or fitted plastic lids on takeaway cappuccinos. But to Meredith this felt like placing the narrowest peg in the widest hole. Maybe Christina was the young woman who stabbed her boyfriend's mother on the same street Meredith lived on, or the mother of the infant who used the stained rickety stroller parked outside the flat below Meredith's. Or she was the Christina who always asked Meredith to cover her shifts at work, giving her hardly any notice and knowing Meredith would always agree.

Dear Christina,

This afternoon I met your old fourth-year teacher, near the bus stops. I said you were fine. Do you remember him? I enclose a little something that I hope you can use wisely. He sent you his best, as do I. Please call, Christina; I would so love to hear your voice just for a moment.

This most recent card gave Meredith pause. For the past three days she had scrabbled her hand into the bank of cold metal post-boxes on the ground floor of her building, reaching and yearning for it. Her first reaction upon finally feeling the rasping paper was annoyance. *What took you so long?* With all my love, Mum. This must be it, Meredith thinks. Time to go.

Oil to run through her black hair, oil to rub into her tough cuticles, oil for her elbows, heels and knees. Her mother taught her that. But what Christina needs, what she craves, is salted, melted butter. On a muffin, on a pancake, on fresh bread, on fresh, warm anything. She'd leave a teaspoonful on her stomach as she lay in the sun and watch it slip down her side if she could. But there's no sun here, so she dreams of stirring it into soup, into a dessert.

The schools closed the year it snowed when her father was here. He wasn't working then; she couldn't remember when he ever ventured from his den in those days. But that day he was dressed, his messy hair was covered with a cap, and he took Christina and two friends sledding. He pulled them along by a rat-tail rope, the wooden runners leaving flattened lines like a wagon trail. At lunch he took them all home for eggs and toast and coffee, put their gloves on the radiator, their socks in the dryer. Someone tutted from the kitchen as he wrapped them back them up again for more time in the snow, but all Christina saw was the swirl of a skirt turning away into the kitchen.

He pulled them, pushed them and dared them down the hills of Dowanhill Park, only stopping when the snow turned orange under the street lights. When he'd dropped them all home, one-by-one, and she was last and lighter, he jogged with her, made the sled go fast. He stopped outside a grand house with a grand drive, untouched by footprints, no marks from birds or animals, just clean and bright. Christina couldn't resist, jumped up and ran circles, pushing down hard to make the snow creak beneath her boots. Panting and looking into his face, he said, 'That's a shame', and she knew she'd ruined something, snapped something, and she was ashamed.

If he was here, could see this rain beating down spring, he'd say something similar. And if her mother knew that she was back here, rubbing butter not oil into her lips, she'd tut.

Meredith puts her plastic potted plants on the other side of her windowsill, leaving them to fend for themselves. She draws the curtains and uses gaffer tape to seal the slit in the metal post-box assigned to her flat. When she walks over the bridge she drops her key into the river, even though this will mean losing her deposit. In her backpack are a grey woollen cardigan, a thin leather belt and a pair of red shoes.

Oor Stany Lantren

Alastair Reid

Pithie larach an shilpie airn,
Auld brie-stane stap slawly wearin',
Feal tae hunners that be gaein'
Towmond an' fit.
Like locus fur a casual gaitherin'
Or a pairt tae steep and sit.

Polisht panel, gleet o' gowd,
Goamin tae the eydent haund.
Paums birse conter, metal cauld.
Docher and weir,
Timmer, daurk an' cannie auld,
Shaks mony luif ootthrou the year.

Treen stair ahead, mirkie and ratchit,
Raiglar lilt o' bauk an' staundart.
Set in the waw, curn airty plantit.
Purrin leam,
Frae a gailerie, kyndly lichtit.
Mynd and ferlie stairt tae gleam.

Wi vyce a-moot an quate gainder
The leebrar is a steid tae hinder.
Yird, lowe, air an' watter,
Oam wauk wae lair.
Beuk an' pairchmet, awid reader,
Unkiver saicrets fae inower.

Two Fat Ladies

Jose Manuel Correa Rollano

It was the first cloudy morning in three weeks, and Glasgow was looking depressing. The rain was battering against the windows of the house where Mrs. Black had been in labour for the last fifteen hours. The summer that was overwhelming the city in a very unusual way appeared to be over because of what was about to happen in the house of the Blacks.

It was 29th of August of 1899. In a beautiful Victorian house, built in sandstone with the Clan's coat of arms above the door, Penelope and Lavender Black were born. Their birth broke their parents' lives in two, not just because it was an unusual phenomenon, but because it caused their mother to flee to the distant hills of paradise, leaving the girls in the sole company of their unfortunate father.

The mother knew she was in labour when her body began to collapse and she had the sudden feeling of life being sucked out of her by the babies, or better said, the baby. Once the girls were out, the mother, knowing she was dying, asked to see the babies and panicked when she did so. The babies were attached by their thorax, each of them having two feet but just one arm in each side of their little body. From the top of the chest two thin necks sustained the heads of the daughters of John Percival Black. The mother, blaming herself for this atrocity, surrendered to death as payment for her sins.

The first years in the lives of Penelope and Lavender Black were quite curious. Even though their father was not proud of them in any aspect, he gave them everything they wanted and needed. Their first steps were difficult as Penelope was always faster than Lavender. The lack of coordination made them fall constantly, provoking the secret laughter of all the family and friends. After some years, the feet were coordinated, but the arms were a nightmare for both, as each of them was in control of just one. It was fine when they took something that was near and easy to carry, but each time they had to work as a team to pick things with both hands, usually the things fell and broke. Most of the time, the victim was the cookie pot. Each time they tried to steal cookies before dinner the porcelain pot fell and broke into a million pieces.

As the years passed, the girls surprisingly transformed into beautiful women. Their bodies might have been attached to each other, but their faces were the most beautiful on Scottish land. They were like Olympian goddesses, whose molten bodies didn't look as weird as one would imagine. Their marble skin and ginger hair gave the impression of seeing Venus reflected in a mirror. Their eyes were like precious stones. Penelope had blue eyes as beautiful and shiny as sapphires. Lavender, on the other hand, honoured her name with purple eyes that resembled a pair of amethysts shining in the sun.

Mr. Black was horrified. Every day the sons of his best friends knocked on the door of the beautiful house asking for his thoughts.

What if one of them falls in love? What if one of them decides to get married? What if one of them has to live as a slave of the other's husband? What if both of them have to live with their husbands together?

Mr. Black was confused and scared for his daughters. The idea that the entire community was busy imagining such scandals was enough to make him sick.

On the girls' sixteenth birthday, Mr. Black held a party at his house, inviting all his friends and their families. The house was full of young men pretending to win the heart of one of the beautiful sisters and young women hating them for being more attractive than them, even though they were considered an abomination of nature. Penelope and Lavender were wearing a white dress decorated with pearls and everyone at the party thought they were watching a beautiful giant swan with two heads. The way they walked was perfect and sublime; every movement was coordinated and harmonious.

After the dinner, two young twin brothers approached them. They talked for hours about mundane topics and laughed at each other's comments, which deteriorated as the night went on and the alcohol took its toll. By midnight the sisters decided to take their young courters to their father's library to have some more privacy – if you could refer to a four-person gathering as "private".

As the alcohol started playing with their heads, the brothers started touching the sisters in inappropriate ways. The sisters were happy to have their first sexual experience and allowed the brothers to take advantage of the situation. The young couples were about to get naked when Mr. Black entered the room. He was petrified, as he saw all of his nightmares come true all at once.

In the name of God! Mr. Black said before falling to the ground.

Those were John Percival Black's last words before suffering a heart attack, dying only a few seconds later. No one ever knew why Mr. Black died that night in such a way and with such a horrible expression on his face.

The young sisters were now on their own in a big and lonely house for just two people who really only occupied the space of one or maybe one and a half people. They lived off the profit made by their father's luxurious restaurant which had given the family a good place in Glasgow's society for years.

After four years of solitude, one morning in the spring of 1919, the two sisters were walking through a park when they caught sight of what they thought was an angel: a young handsome man, with blond hair, eyes as green as emeralds, and a muscular appearance. They were both staggered and their heart almost stopped when the man responded to them with a smile. Yes! Their heart! Inside all that mixture of muscles and bones there was just one heart. One heart to share, one heart to live, and one heart to feel.

The young man was enchanted. He couldn't believe his eyes. Two beautiful women inseparably attached to each other who stared at him like birds of prey.

Good morning ladies. – The young man said. – I am Dimitri Steklov.

You must be Russian, right? – Lavender asked.

Yes my lady, I am indeed. I am escaping from my homeland to avoid a bullet crashing through my head. These are bad times back there.

Well if that is the case, let us welcome you to Glasgow, Mr. Steklov, Penelope said with a naughty expression in her eyes.

After a couple of weeks of getting to know each other, the sisters offered Dimitri a room in their house, paying no mind to the neighbours' comments and the criticism of their father's friends. The feeling in their heart was too strong to behave prudently when Dimitri was around.

A year later, Dimitri was in charge of the restaurant and he was, in all manners, behaving like their husband. Even though the church did not officially marry them, they were husband and wives in every possible way. One morning the sisters awoke to find their man surprisingly gone. The letter he had left on the kitchen table read:

'My lovely women, I had to urgently go to Russia; I will be back in a month with my sister.

Always yours,

Dimitri.'

After a couple of days alone, the sisters felt annoyed by the lack of sex and the feeling of solitude, constantly reminding them of Dimitri's absence.

You know what, Lavender? – said Penelope in a very provocative tone.

What! – replied Lavender aggressively.

I am tired of smelling your shit! You should stop eating that much so I don't have to go with you to the toilet all the time!

What? You are the one who eats like a pig and I never complain about the smell! – replied Lavender, feeling insulted.

Well I don't think so! If things were like that, Dimitri would not be in a relationship with us! Don't you understand he is here because he loves me? You are just an additive to our love. – Penelope said that with such anger that her eyes looked like vipers spitting poison.

Shut up! – Lavender screamed.

And what if I don't?

Well I am going to eat like a real pig so you have to come with me to the bathroom at least seven times a day!

You wouldn't do such a thing. – Penelope said.

Well, watch me!

Lavender ate amazing amounts of food that week and Penelope was the one who was feeling the necessity to go to the toilet all the time. By Sunday Penelope noticed that her legs, arm and neck were getting fat.

I don't understand! I ate almost nothing this week and now I am gaining weight. – Penelope said looking at her half of the body reflected in the mirror.

Well you should learn from me! I ate like a pig and look; I am as thin as last week!

Everything was clear now. Lavender was eating and it was Penelope who was gaining the weight.

Well, when Dimitri comes back and sees us like this, he will think you are as fat as me! – Penelope screamed to Lavender.

Three weeks later, both sisters were as fat as a cow and their movements were very slow and awkward. One morning the mail brought another letter from Dimitri:

'My lovely women,

I have to speak the truth. I am in Rome right now and I will not come back. I met the love of my life on my way to Russia.

I am very sorry my loves and I will always remember our times together. Thank you for everything.

Always yours,

Dimitri.'

Penelope and Lavender were flabbergasted. The idea of never seeing Dimitri again drove them crazy. They went to the kitchen and in the middle of a panic attack they started to eat everything they saw on the table and in the cupboards. They ate through the night and into the next day. After many hours of eating, the oxygen stopped passing through Lavender's throat. She realized that she wasn't breathing, but that her heart was still beating. In that moment she knew once again that there was just one heart in that shared body. The feeling of love was shared by both twins and there was no reason to fight over it; the man they loved was one and the same man. Penelope stopped breathing too and realized that the smell of shit she had been complaining about was her own smell, as it was her food that Lavender processed each time they ate. Those minutes of revelations were the last revelations of the sisters. Their eyes became cloudy as their souls left their body, and they moved on to meet their parents on the other side.

Two years later, Dimitri choked to death on an olive while he was having lunch.

Poor are those who hurt the ones who love them most, because sooner or later life will take revenge on them.

Helen Kellock

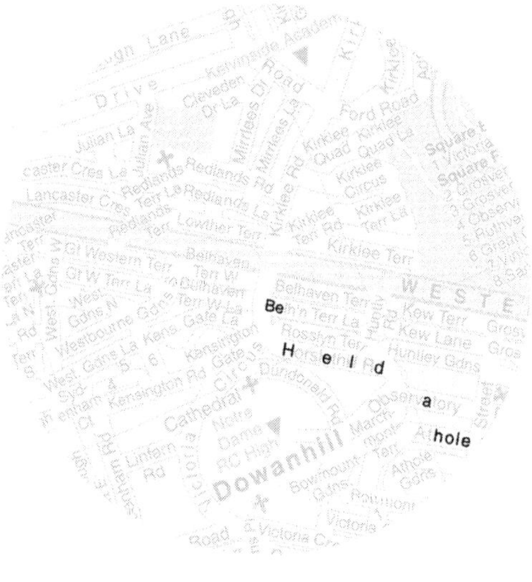

Helen Kellock

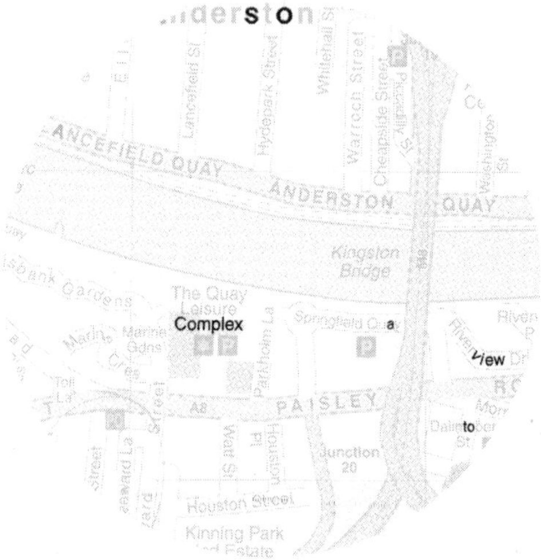

A Strange Story About Spiders

Eleanor Morton

Last year I moved from St. Andrews to Glasgow, after transferring my university course, and agreed to share the flat with an old school friend, who had already been at Glasgow Uni for a couple of years. We found a pretty suitable place, one of those typical Glaswegian red-stone tenement flats, really close to the university, and on the third floor, so we wouldn't have to worry about burglary, as my flatmate had done in her last place.

The flat itself was nothing special; two bedrooms, a living room, bathroom and cabin kitchen was pretty adequate for the two of us plus her boyfriend, who usually stayed over. The carpets and walls were a rather unflattering green, and in need of a good clean (or better yet, complete removal), but neither of us was fussy. In short, it was fine, and close enough to the shops and the subway to keep us happy.

One rather dark, damp November morning we both woke up very late, and then lounged around the sitting room for several hours, all of our lectures having been cancelled due to a strike. My flatmate mentioned having a very strange dream in the night – so strange, in fact, that she had woken up and leapt from the bed. She had dreamt, she said, that she had woken up to find two spiders in the bed, running between her and her boyfriend. 'They were really horrible' she said, squirming at the memory, but (being a maths student) didn't elaborate on the description. When her boyfriend came in later, he confirmed that she had indeed leapt from the bed that morning, pointing to the covers, obviously still dreaming, although he checked the mattress to make sure. I didn't think much of it, other than it was more exciting than most of the dreams I'd been having lately, which mostly involved humiliating myself in public with various cooking implements.

But a few days later, alone in the flat, I was washing my hands in the bathroom when I felt something soft brush past my foot. Looking down, I was horrified to see a gigantic spider sidling under the sink. Letting out a sort of breathy whimper, I curled my toes away in horror. It was unlike any other spider

I had ever seen. It had the round chunky body of a tarantula, all eyes and bony pincers, but the legs were quite disturbing – they were large and elongated like the stuffed spider crabs I'd seen at the Scottish Museum, curving up and outwards from the body. The oddest thing, however, was the colour, for the whole thing was a sickly yellowish white, and covered in silvery hairs. Its eyes were shiny and painfully red. The horrible entity was about the size of both of my hands, and moved at an alarming rate, crawling (and how it fitted I still can't comprehend) into a small crack between the bath and the walls. Within a few seconds it had gone, though it took me another ten minutes before I could move. I'm afraid of spiders at the best of times, and this incident left me feeling as though someone had smashed me round the head with a bottle of vodka.

By the time my flatmate came back several hours later, I had managed to make a cup of tea, and she found me sitting with both feet tucked up on a chair in the middle of the living room. I told her what had happened, and we concluded that, due to exams, the coldness of the flat, and the amount of sugar I'd consumed that day, I must surely have had some sort of stress-induced hallucination. What's more, the species of spider I had seen didn't even exist, as a quick internet search verified. I *must*, therefore, have made it up. I must have.

So imagine my horror, three days later, when I opened my wardrobe and found a huge pale spider hanging by a pale leg from one of my jumpers, turning very slowly whilst producing a sticky web from its throbbing body. It dropped almost immediately into the darkness below, between some jackets and a suitcase. A tentative search revealed nothing. Perhaps, I reasoned, the whole thing had been some sort of prolonged delirium; but even so, I didn't open the wardrobe for another week.

After my flatmate ran screaming from the shower one Friday, shrieking that there was 'a massive white insect' clinging to the shower curtain, we decided to call a pest remover, since it had obviously gone beyond hallucinations. But although he did find traces of mice in the kitchen, the spiders were nowhere to be found.

From then on these beasts would appear every so often throughout the flat. Typically, we wouldn't have seen any for weeks, and then suddenly one would scuttle out from behind the kitchen bin, or from under the coffee table. My friend's boyfriend once picked up a magazine and found one lurking beneath, its legs tucked up at odd angles beneath it, abdomen pulsating. My flatmate nearly squashed one with the kettle when it appeared from behind the bread bin, and managed to splash hot water over it – she said it made an odd, shrill whistling sound as it fled. I once opened the oven to find one crawling slowly along the grill, its legs tangled awkwardly between the metal bars. By the time I'd picked up the baking tray that'd been dropped in fright, it had disappeared.

The oddest thing about these Animals is that they seemed to disappear within seconds of being sighted. Once I caught one creeping through my underwear drawer. I slammed it shut again and managed to lock the eight-legged voyeur inside. When my friend returned from lectures, I triumphantly revealed my catch to her, but the glorified opening of the drawer showed only a couple of pairs of off-white pants and a threadbare bra. The only thing revealed that day was that I was in dire need of new clothes. My friend was unimpressed. Which brings me to the other oddity in the story – try as we might, we could never witness one together. Either my flatmate, her boyfriend, or I would spot one, but never when we were together, and as soon as we yelled to each other, the spider would have somehow have escaped in the few seconds our heads were turned.

I was never in any doubt that there was more than one. Somehow, I seemed to know that each was a different Thing, with its own personality. One of them, I noticed, as it darted underneath my bed clumsily, seemed to have an odd lopsided limp, as if a few of its legs had been slammed in a door. There was another considerably larger than the rest, which tucked itself into one of my hats when I tossed it onto the floor. Luckily I spotted it before I had a chance to put it back on my head. One night I awoke very sweaty and panicked for no reason, and my eyes were drawn to the other end of the room, where I saw three lumpy shadows creeping across the high ceiling. I regarded them moving rapidly towards me, until one seemed to slip and fall, and the others followed, sliding down the wall and into the darkness. Instinctively putting my hands up, I felt a stinging running down the back of my hand before all three spiders disappeared. Of course, when I switched on my light, there was nothing to be seen, but the thin scratch it had left on my hand stayed there for a good three days afterwards. The only thing usual about it was that it was a vivid blue colour and itched when I washed my hands.

I began to experience horrible 'night terrors' after that – extreme anxiety attacks in my sleep – and would wake up breathing rapidly and clenching my fists. This was followed by a sense of paranoia, that unease you get in a shop when you mistake the clothes mannequin behind you for another customer. The kitchen began to feel like a no-go zone, filling with a horrible smoky smell that lingered for several hours at a time, and I found myself turning quickly whenever I was alone in the flat, switching on all the lights and turning up the radio. My flatmate told me she had once been making tea in the kitchen when she noticed a dark figure standing in the vestibule, blurrily outlined by the glass door. She called out to them, but after she'd turned back from putting the butter knife down, they had somehow gone.

But the event that startled me the most must have been the incident one Tuesday, about three months after the first beastie had appeared. As I was lying in bed, listening to the rain thudding dully against the window, I became aware of an odd shuffling near the door and lifted myself slightly to peer over the end of the bed. In a stain of moonlight (I always keep the curtain open; it helps me to get up early), two of the spiders, positively glowing in the bright beam, their hairs sticking up and outlining their ugly crabbish shapes, were dragging something between them. This object, I realised, was a human hand, removed just above the wrist, and very fresh looking. It might have been a child's hand, as I remember it was quite small and white, with small, round nails. The spiders were slowly devouring it, chewing away at the soft skin, their fat greasy pincers digging in, one finger already gone. They were rapid in their work, all the while making this horrible squishy noise, as they chomped through the meat. At that point I think I started to shout, something like 'stop it!' and found myself quite awake, shrinking in the sudden daylight, with the duvet on the floor.

After six months or so, the Things disappeared, the last one I recall seeing having dropped from the underside of my desk one afternoon and landing quite close to my foot. We stayed in that flat another three months, before moving to share with another friend who had come back from teaching in France. The new flat had no ghostly tarantulas, only ants in the kitchen, none of which I ever saw eating anything other than my fruit. A month or so later I was waiting in a café for my History tutor, and struck up a conversation with a man who (I thought I recognized him) still lived in the flat two floors below the one where all this had happened. It's an odd footnote, but I have to mention the renovation work he was describing to me.

'They took up all the floor in your flat after the new guy complained, and found something wedged in between the pipes'.

'What?' I asked

'Something rotten, an animal, a piece of meat… It was fuckin' horrible, I saw them removing it in a plastic bag. Looked like it had fingers. The smell…'

Sometimes I think I ought to go to the library, or the council, or wherever it is that they might keep public records or notes about certain incidents. But I wouldn't know where to begin. Or when. Or what, if anything, I was actually looking for. Sometimes I wish the entire event ought to have a nice clean ending to it, an explanation, a conclusion. But I don't know if I want to go looking for it. I don't know what those spiders were. I once read that dreams about spiders are a manifestation of an unknown fear. Sometimes it felt to me as if the flat itself was scared of something. Or someone. I don't know. For now I'd rather just remember it as a strange story about spiders.

Ghost, Charing Cross

Eleanor Stewart

Honest tae God,
spittin image;
Donald Dewar
staunin at the lights
waitin tae cross.

Watt Brothers

Eleanor Stewart

Dinnae be wastin money
on they big knittin needles.
Buy a couple ae broom handles;
get yer man
tae sharpen the ends.

Byelaws

Eleanor Stewart

According to the sign,
skate boarding and
roller skating are
prohibited
outside Scotland's
premier
lap dancing club.

It's an offence.

Containing Itself

Michael Strain

So, it was dark. Well, dark to me anyway. I suppose if I could've seen the dull radiation floating around since the dawn of time it might have been a different story. Me, I could only see those little flashes of red and blue in the black. So, mostly, it was dark. Then again, I say 'it' was dark, but when I wasn't exchanging the odd photon with the cosmos, 'I' was dark. It was a bit like being punched awake. Bang. Photon. Nothing. Bang, another photon. Stop. Were there long vast swathes of time between each event? I don't know, it could just as easily have been only brief instants. The universe could have been deconstructed and rebuilt between my epiphanies. Who knew, it had no bearing on my binary experiences anyway. On or off. I was just dust in a strobe light. Let's say then that the flashes got faster. It meant nothing to me of course, I had no in-between, but the on moments began to have a bit more detail. On. Nothing. On, waitasecondisthatanotheroneon. Off. Flash. Icouldswearit'sgettingwarmer. Silence. Bang. Bloodyhellthat'sbright,therem ustbe. I'm paraphrasing right enough; at that point I was all just tick tock tick tock, bright dark. All the 'Bloody hell' nonsense I'm just kind of guessing at. Maybe the collection of 'Ons' felt like that. Maybe they were what feelings were made of. I don't know. But at some stage the nothings stopped. Light was streaming in from everywhere. Distances started to make sense, sizes and positions. I could differentiate between things, things and myself. One point in particular was interesting. Denser than the others, like I could reach out and toy with it, pick at it to see what spilled out. It was moving fast too. Moving. That was another one I had to get used to. I had to keep track, to see where things were going, what they were all bumping into. That's when I started the catalogue. Trying to keep it all in order. It was all about the relationships. Relative positions, exchanges, interstellar shenanigans. Connections. But that wee bit of it, the wee clump on the right was getting bigger. Bigger or closer? It was still difficult to tell in those days. Maybe it was me getting smaller. That didn't tally though, with the catalogue I mean. After all, the number of entries was getting bigger, and I must have had somewhere to mark it all down. Definitely closer.

I don't know what I thought would happen. You've got to remember that at that stage all the collisions I'd been involved in had been pretty gentle. I mean, there's not that much kick off of a photon. This thing was big though. Massive. Mind you, as I got nearer, or as it got nearer, or as we got nearer, it did spread out a bit. More stars. Big gaps. Maybe I could just shoodle through one of the spaces. Then, all of a sudden, right mid-count of what I later learned to be a particularly unimportant group of helium atoms on one of the spiral arms, it hits me. Light, heat, energy, solid mass, whatever you want to call it, it's all the same to me. Nevertheless, bang, pretty much covers the experience.

Result, here's me bathed in so much activity, so many atoms, so much light, I don't know where to start counting. But that's the only way to see what's going on right? Now, I could've got completely overwhelmed at this stage, I mean you really have no idea the amount of crap that was flying about that place. But I got focussed in a bit. The low grey ceiling over it all was quite effective in forcing attention down, making you forget about the vast mess above it. And let's face it, how do you catalogue it *all*? You have to make a note of it somewhere. Before you know it, you've got a few million pages done, and that's only about the ink on the first letter. I mean seriously, if you want to make a map of the whole thing you're going to need the whole thing to write it with. And the catalogue just becomes the thing itself. You can't just fold it all up and keep it in just a wee corner of itself. Even I know that much. But take a slice, focus in. That, I can just about manage, and it's funny, turns out a lot of it looks the same.

Anyway, here's me. It's bright, well brighter than before, big grey sky and a mass of exciting new interactions. So I start with the electrons, easy to see, not so interesting though, all very alike. Too many. Limit the catalogue more, a bit at a time. Tighter boundaries. No need to rush. So I started to count groups. Arrangements. Hexagonal rings of them, triangular lattices. All alike, all just a little bit boring. Let's just skip it. Let's just say I spent too much time counting bloody atoms. Forest, trees? Not lost on me, okay?

So finally, there I was, floating about, checking out the big picture. Organic molecules, now we're talking, life, organisms. Something to watch shimmying along, doing things. Catching the scents coming out of the disused rail tunnels under the streets, long forgotten. Or watching rays of light from the distant ball of gas ricochet off of glaring aluminium waves, mirroring the river beside them. Actually, it turns out eyeballs are a great place to sit. Lots of information, though they do focus on the strangest things just when you're getting interested in something else. I tried a few. Views of bevelled stone columns under blankets of Christmas lights, large rectangles of grass bending under thousands of singing voices, heavy raindrops bouncing from red sandstone to thick rhododendron leaves. I might have tried something different at that point, untangled myself from the dark streets and leafy pavements, hidden basement flats and soot stained brickwork. However, I caught a glimpse of something from the corner of the eye I was in. It was a cathedral tower, but reflected in a huge glass wall. The light had bounced twice from the sun before hitting me, so what was I looking at here, the glass, the cathedral, the sun? They were all connected, true, but the meaning was in the reflections. Then it occurred to me that I was not at the end of these things. Who knew what layers I hadn't plumbed yet? I watched a yellow ray of light hit the retina beside me and latched onto the pulse of energy it released, spiralling back into the vast web of reflections that still I can't believe I hadn't noticed before. I bounced through the spongy mass, optic nerve, frontal cortex, up and over the top, lines, motions, electrical discharge. I'd catalogued these things of course, like the river or the crazy paving of bridges over it, but never from the inside. I thought they were all pretty much the same. All electrical connections, discharges, blockages and blood. All nice and causal. All similar. But inside! It was like the galaxy all over again. Bang, bang, bang! That's my problem, too short-sighted. We passed a pub beside the park. I got the images of the stone, the liquids hidden from view, the bright noise and heat. Then, broadsided. A whole rake of action I'd overlooked. Triggered from the outside, but not reflecting it at all. I followed the forms, collated the input. Another reflection, another façade, from lower down, duller clothes, denser black stains on the stonework. Another reflection, but in time, amalgamated with this one. I could feel the sense of it as it washed around me. A shadow flitted behind the concentration. Something else, brief, but gone now. I was shocked, struggled a bit, and moved to another body nearby. Almost the same signals in, but the reflections in time were gone, replaced. The place looked different from here, less foreboding, jolly even. Same thing in, different thing out. Another shadow bloomed briefly before evaporating. So I decided to stick around, explore things from the inside, these multiple views, overlaid onto what I thought was only one.

I lurked at the top of the hill in the park, looking down over spires, cranes and the shining band of the river. I jumped from mind to mind. Let them pass through my vantage point and watched as the view metamorphosed in front of me, feeling the intangible atmosphere inside. Buildings grew and shrank in their spots as they were tied back in time with each set of connections. Colours wavered, the whole thing vanished at the touch of a companion's hand, internal worlds overwhelming the outside. And always the shifting shadows I couldn't latch onto, diffracting around the neurons. Vague senses of heat or cold, repulsion or attraction. Then the mind would be carried from my spot and the next would arrive creating a new world around me. It was incredible, to see the very fabric of the universe change without actually doing anything. But these bodies could take that vision and impose it over the other world. Their actions moulding the external mass of particles into their own view of it.

I wanted to see more. I wanted to see all of the items of the catalogue shift and slide around this new gravitational pull. I travelled with them, but it took too long first hand. They read. I saw that they were cataloguers too. Taking slices of what they saw and trying to tie it down. The multi-storey bookshops and domed libraries held the fossils of these thoughts weighed down in ink and heavy cream pages. I traversed them, mired in the contradictions, feeling the absence of the shadows in the gaps they left between words. Worlds within worlds blossomed and died as I tried to absorb it all. But I couldn't reconcile them. Not without the envelope of experience. Not without the direct onslaught of past, present and desired future. The pages told the story, but they lacked the force of the thing, the belief in each of these realities. They fell too easily, the worlds flimsy and inconsistent.

I drifted for a while after that, always moving, mind to mind. Chasing shadows. As a maker of lists, I suppose I was always on a hiding to nothing. The potential was infinite. Too many cities, too many real variations of the place. The shadows dancing within those images, colouring their shades, nudging action, stepping lightly ahead.

I could say 'suddenly', but that was exactly the problem. 'Suddenly' I was unsure of time. I had been hitching lifts on rapidly effervescing particles, beams of light and matter, connecting all of the little trips I made. I had seen so much, so many invisible cities. I had floated on waves of sound from tenement bands, caught on thermals of old bar heaters and latched onto glinting rays from lead windows, flitting through the light drizzle and back into another infinitely variable reflection. What if I was just on some short trajectory then? I was bouncing through this place until entropy pulled us apart and I became the same old switch in the darkness. Who knew which leap would rip me from the arms of the dear green place I now inhabited. I followed the light, the particles connecting. Everything was connecting. Existing only to connect. What about me? Am I on-route then? Am I just waiting to connect, a complex path between two points? Ready to be annihilated on arrival, the transport of information, transformed at a destination, or is my trajectory the thing? Everything has its antithesis, its destruction. Mine must be waiting out there, and here am I chasing shadows. They, like me, drifting past the interactions that only weakly see us. Are they my end? Point to point, waiting to meet the darkness again, or finally to turn and see the shadow of reflection.

Dog Fowling

Cedric Tai

Sitting round and new, broken in parts

a reward is printed on fliers, invisible to the creature that left me on this concrete a reward for spying on your neighbors

a different initiative could've been enacted, a neighborhood poop pickup day, a street cleaning tax,

but obviously nothing of the sort happens,

because I'm still here

I dry out over weeks
after the flies pick out the nutrients and fly away,
the rest streaming down the sidewalk back into the earth fertilizing nothing in particular

This empty shell isn't going anywhere

Visually reanimated by the rain,
I don't float,
don't move,
don't budge

People quick on their feet dodge, just in time
but that gets tiring after a while,
so when you let your guard down
it's just a game of luck.

For those who really stopped caring, the length of me is spread out as long as the sidewalk and then I might finally disappear

but that hasn't happened yet either,

because I'm still here

here along the edge of a sidewalk, with another one, a different one, not more than five meters away

and still two more of us before the end of the block.
but because of proximity they're not my friends,

we are the same, but we're in our own places, no,

my closest companions are

a Walker chips bag against a fence,

some new light-colored vomit that's really much more in the way
but farther along to being spread thin into a long nothingness

and some non-descript black clothing in a puddle that used to be in an alley around the corner,
which seems ridiculous that this heavy unwanted thing gets around more than I do,

I at least can be kicked to the drainage,
or tossed under the bushes,

but, I'm still here

Glasgow II

Suzanne Muir Scott

what is it, in Glasgow
in the gloaming, when
the air is crisp and
cold this October?

perhaps it is the
lighted windows,
curtains not yet shut
and the bare West
End floorboards
comfy chairs and
chessboards.

perhaps it is my
heart, affected and
sad
with too much
deliberation and too
much life had.

what is it, in the
city, just before

Wee Man

James Malcolm

They lived in a Gorbals block called Spence Tower. When John's gran moved in to look after him and Anne, she bought him a boy's suit for his father's funeral. The cuffs reached his knuckles, and the lapels brushed his chin when he sat down, but she said he should have a proper wee suit and that he'd grow into it. He was the man of the house, now.

When they got home John took a claw hammer from his father's toolbox. He ripped his bedroom carpet back from the skirting and pried up one of the floorboards. The shallow space beneath was safe and just big enough for the little brown paper parcel. John knew from the shape that it was a toy car. It was his father's best work. He put the floorboard back and tacked the carpet into place.

John grew up and went to work in construction. He took work where he could find it. A year working forestry in Canada. A short career on the North Sea Oil Rigs. Six months construction in Abu-Dhabi. He kept paying the rent on the flat however far he travelled, no matter how thin it stretched his paycheques. He returned to Glasgow on the 31st December after being laid off from another crew. Anne met him at international arrivals. He looked pale and exhausted. When she gave him a hug, he winced.

'Can I see?' She asked.

John lifted his jumper to show her the bandages taped over his left side from belly button to ribcage and the mottled bruising around the edges. Anne sucked air through her teeth.

'Let's get you home.'

They ran out to the car through the weather, and John insisted on driving. Anne rubbed his shoulder as he guided the car onto the motorway.

'Don't let this get you down. There's no shame in it.'

'It wasn't my fault.'

'No. Listen, why don't we drive straight back to my house? You can spend the evening with me and Gary and the kids. Watch the bells on telly, have some champagne.'

John couldn't stand the thought of spending Hogmanay around Gary.

Anne kept trying to cheer him up. 'Just take some time before you figure out what to do next, eh?'

'What do you mean? I'm going back out, Anne. There's more work.'

Anne took her hand away from John's shoulder, and stared at the road.

'This is the work I do. It's just tough times. People get laid off.'

Anne poked is stomach, and he yelped.

'Not for no reason.' She said. 'Why don't you try another line of work?'

John gripped the steering wheel tightly.

'It was good enough for Dad; it's good enough for me.'

'It wasn't good enough for Dad. We could only ever afford to live in that shitty flat.'

'It was a step up for him. He was born in a single-end.'

'Was he fuck!'

But he was. He was real Glasgow. And he worked on the shipyards and he had a mother who washed the clothes in the steamie on Tuesdays. It was all real. A past so close you could feel its breath on the back of your neck.

The traffic closed in around them as they drew up to the Kingston Bridge.

'I'd rather be alone tonight, Anne.'

'Come stay with us.'

'Drop it, Anne. I'm going to the flat.'

'You can't.' There was an odd insistence in her voice.

'Why not?'

'Pull over, we should talk about this.'

'Traffic's not moving, tell me now.'

Anne straightened up in her seat. Probably best to break the news quickly.

'Tower's being demolished. They cleared out the last of the tenants last week. Some of your things are with me, the rest is in storage.'

John rubbed his temples and stared at the faded little airbag logo in the middle of the steering wheel.

'I didn't want you to be worrying about it while you were away. I know how you get. You can stay with me and Gary as long as you like, ok?'

John thought of the bedroom carpet. Of the loose patch under the bed, and the treasure stowed underneath.

'Did you move everything out?'

'Yes, everything.'

'No, you didn't.'

'We did, John.'

He turned to her and yelled. 'You didn't!'

Anne shrank back.

'How dare you not tell me! It's our family home, Anne. How dare you!'

He turned back to the road and gripped the steering wheel. The traffic started to worm forwards through the bridge. He drove on. Anne stared into the distance and he felt like a monster. He was sweating, his mouth was trembling. He tried to steady himself and speak evenly.

'I'm sorry.'

Anne clenched her fists. 'Don't ever shout at me like that.'

'I said I was sorry.'

John's knuckles clicked as he gripped the wheel tighter. He wasn't going to say anything else. He should just stop talking now.

'You should be happy to be rid of that place.'

'Fuck!'

He slammed his fist into the steering wheel. Anne grabbed him.

'John!'

He shook her off, opened his door, and stepped out into the clogged motorway. Drivers tooted their horns and Anne screamed after him. He kept walking and didn't look back.

Anne went to open her door and run after him, but the traffic was starting to move. She called for him again.

'John, get back here!'

The car was clogging the centre lane, drivers leant on their horns and yelled coarse insults out their windows. Anne climbed over into the driver's seat and moved the car forward. She looked for her brother but he was already gone.

Spence Tower was ringed with rickety construction fences and guarded from a single wee portacabin nestled into the south wall of the building. Inside, a doddery security guard dozed in front of a television playing Jackie Bird and Celtic Connections. John strolled right past him.

He paused outside the main door and looked up. The power was out and the tower's dark silhouette leaned over him. Inside the lobby it was freezing cold and smelt like plaster dust. He couldn't see more than a few feet into the darkness. He took out his mobile and shone a pale light on his path. With the lifts out he'd have to take the stairwell. The light in front of him flickered and his phone vibrated with an incoming call from Anne. He ignored it and kept using the phone as a torch.

When he entered the stairwell he saw broken walls, exposed pipes. They were well into preparing the building for demolition. He sprinted up the stairs. Two, three at a time. His guts burned and he thought of blood and burst stitches. When he reached his floor he was ready to throw up back down the stairwell, but he stood straight and bore the pain.

It was still dark, but there was only a single corridor running the length of the building, and John knew his way. He found his flat and fumbled for keys out of habit, but the door was ajar. John stepped inside, and saw that his flat was already gone.

The internal partitions had been removed for the demolition, leaving empty space running the length of the building. You could mark the places where homes used to be by a patchwork of clashing wallpaper surviving on the outer walls. The glass had been taken out of the windows, and some of the outer panels had been removed and the floor ended in sheer empty space. Freezing wind blew through the building, bringing the rain with it.

John looked for the outline of his flat on the floor and ceiling. Familiar lino. Scraps of his carpets. A single hardy strand of flypaper clung to the ceiling where the kitchen used to be. He walked through the living room wall to the bedroom, got down on his knees and started prying at the loose floorboard. His phone was ringing again.

He had almost got purchase on it when he heard footsteps approach down the corridor. The next door down opened, and Anne stepped through, holding her mobile.

'Hey neighbour. Answer your phone.'

John stopped prying at the floorboard.

'Let me help.'

'I've got it.'

The board flexed up and Anne got her fingers underneath it. She yanked back, and it snapped in a puff of dust and a sound like a gunshot. It was made of cheap laminate. John was already reaching into the space beneath the floor.

He pulled out the bundle and stripped the paper away. Inside, the wee toy truck was preserved. John had expected it to be rusted, but it was as shiny as the day he hid it away.

Anne looked at it. 'Did Dad make that?'

'Just before he died. It's got a clockwork motor in it.'

'Why did you hide it away?'

'Thanks for moving my stuff out, Anne.'

Now that he was holding it in his hands, the car seemed different. John wound it up and placed it on the floor. It scooted towards the edge of the building. Anne went to grab it, but John stopped her. It ran off the edge, and tumbled away.

Outside, fireworks lit the sky. Cheers wafted over the Clyde from the party in the city centre. Anne hugged her brother.

'Happy New Year.'

John stayed with Anne, Gary and his nephews in their flat further west on the banks of the Clyde. People called these new tower blocks 'apartment buildings', and there were flowers planted in the window boxes. A few weeks later, demolition crews lit the fuse on Spence Tower. Crowds gathered to watch the building disappear in a puff of smoke.

process a k – excerpt three

Samuel Devereux

two chairs a man in each both elderly

1:say do you prefer kelvin or celsius

0:well

0:scratches chin frowns pauses

the room they occupy reveals itself it is small has two windows behind the chairs each window has a pair of curtains the curtains are open there is one door next to the door sit two bins the bins involuntarily shake at unspecified times

1:kelvin i prefer kelvin

0:yes me too

0:scratches chin frowns pauses

1:stands up from chair walks behind it and rests elbows on its back
1:you see kelvin is an absolute scale, it is one of seven base units in the
1:international system of units

0:scratches chin frowns pauses
0:yes that is true it is

1:stops resting on the back of chair and strolls towards one window pauses turns
1:to face chairs
1:it is defined as 1/273.16 of the thermodynamic temperature of the triple point of
1:water

1:turns to face window looks out of window and then closes curtains
1:darkening the room turns back to face chairs

0:yes of course
0:scratches chin frowns pauses

1:walks across room to the second window turns looks out of window holds edge 1:of windowpane

1:its funny how the primary measurement of temperature in physical sciences
1:as defined and discovered via the triple point of water is itself ultimately named
1:after a mass of water that flowed close to a physicists laboratory

0:scratches chin frowns pauses

0:yes

0:turns looks backwards towards the second window remaining seated
0:scratches chin frowns pauses

0:it is as if something has begun to acknowledge itself

1:continues looking out of window

Within Glasgow... Within Me...

Maria Ioana Marchidanu

It's strange how you expect a new city to make you feel lost and alone, when the truth is, it is the place where you find yourself for the first time. You learn how to let feelings grow inside you, feelings that set your soul free like the last mustangs that dance with the wind on green, wild fields.

For me, Glasgow is not a spot you find on a map, but a land where umbrellas make rainbows on the wet pavement. Glasgow is not a place for a honeymoon, but a park where people fall in love. Glasgow is not an ensemble of houses and flats and parking lots, but a forest filled with 'Bambi' characters, an ocean where music, theatre and literature reveal their hidden treasures, a desert where art galleries become a refreshing oasis. Glasgow is the inspiration one finds when writing a novel and, at the same time, the place where fiction becomes reality. 'The wonderful green place' is the stage where I learnt to tango passionately with the wind, dance the rumba in the shivering embrace of fog, experiment the contemporary dance under the rain.

If this Scottish city were a Renaissance collage, the landscape would be a study by Leonardo, its population would be captured in a ballet show by Degas and the chiaroscuro between the sanctity of architectural silence and the ecstatic movement of nightlife would be signed by Rembrandt. If Glasgow were a cup of tea, this would be poured in white porcelain, with pink and purple Japanese flowers left to grow across the cup and plate. If Glasgow were a photograph, then it would capture life and music, poetry and lovers, familiar neighbourhoods and children. And if Glasgow were a novel, it would resemble giant treasures like 'War and Peace' and 'Three Comrades' What is more, this amazingly challenging city leaves its mark in your sweetest memories, as well as in your imagination. Here, your unknown talents and courage take flight and you learn to listen to the sound of quiet breaths. Here, you learn to see extraordinary people in any abstract shapes and shadows.

One Tuesday afternoon, I saw a tree turn into a Jamaican woman, with exotic jewellery and a melancholic expression. Her red and yellow locks of hair were cut off by the storm. Her stingy breasts were symmetrically moving with the chocolate-like hips. This woman had been waiting for her lover for centuries and she was going to wait for more to come. She was not 'The Lady of Shalott', she was Guinevere, she was Desdemona, she was Aphrodite. Her body was rough and almost burning. Her arms and legs were the branches, covered in tattoos and tribal bracelets. In that park, for a few moments, that tree resembled every woman whose eye colour swims through salty tears of happiness before her wedding day. That tree, graciously losing its balance because of the November wind, looked so much like the fair Joan of Arc, shivering at the loss of her innocence.

In Glasgow, the parks are a shape of Eden whose heart holds secrets of freedom and grace, stories about the last wild creatures. In these lands, the grass is as fresh as the summer breeze brought by the waves on the Ancient Greek islands, while the sky is the ballroom for all sublime wings to dance upon. The river's song is a ballad about the patriot warriors whose courage and passion are still reminded of all around us. As I found myself strolling between magnificent trees whose spirit has been guarding Glasgow for centuries, I remembered that man's purpose is to become one with Nature, protecting her. I was reminded of this lesson in Glasgow.

It was in Glasgow still that I found out that a city can make two people fall in love. In this sacred place, all frontiers of age and culture and preconceived ideas become phantasmagorical memories and all that is left is the truest and most purifying feeling of devotion. Here is where I embraced one moment, which went by faster than the blink of an eye, when I felt the wind on the highest peak and the salt of the bluest wave although I was still in bed and the storm was punching my window like a thousand warriors. Here is where I have found one being, one heartbeat, one breath against my cheek that I had been searching for in all the other beings but I never thought I would actually find. I would call it 'beautiful', but it's just a word... You can't really call it anything. I'd want to scream it, but it's so peaceful. I'd want to be quiet, but it's pure ecstasy. I found myself laughing and crying and laughing again. Indeed, I was crying because if I didn't, the colour from my eyes would have melted and would have run through my veins and killed my happiness. All I knew was that I was wishing for that being to feel at least as much as I felt with just one heartbeat. All I can truly explain is that I would have had no more air if I hadn't told that soul how much I was in love with him and how it hurts and it tickles at the same moment, at the same blink of an eye. Thus, Glasgow is the city where I learnt to let go of my fright and peacefully allow my hand to be held by someone who would never let it go.

I cannot begin to explain how I have had the privilege of understanding that a city can make you blossom by teaching you to respect yourself, to trust other people's unconditional friendship and love, to fully live every storm and sunshine and to laugh at the grey sky. Glasgow has given me a spiritual home without expecting anything in return.

My plan to begin again in a place where I would be alone and cold has turned out to be the best time of my life in a land where I have found my place in Nature, society and within myself. So, it is only fair to say that Glasgow has introduced me to my true self.

Maggot

Julie Ramage

Dirty boy, dirty boy, dirty boy
Maggot
Language
I said 'Maggot'
Shut it
I said 'MAGGOT'
Aye, you said it three times-
Gonnae shut it!

Dad, can we get a chip roll?
It's a roll & chips
Chip roll
It's a roll & chips
Chip roll
Roll & chips
Chip roll
Aye, but you're fae Fife, I'm fae Glasgae

Am No A Zombie – Dunnae Call Me Boab

Graham Cee Campbell

Am no a Zombie please dunnae call me Boab
I tell ye – I cannae be
It makes nae sense yah mawkit git
Am no a dippy, dopey duppy monster.
You see, fuh me, white is the colour of darkness
Am no a Zombie please dunnae call me Boab
because Spooks is a spy drama – no' a black guy
Am no a ghost – that's a white Texan dancer
a Mullet-heided chancer contacting his girlfriend
via a potters wheel fae the ither side
Am no a Zombie – will ya jis stop callin me Boab!
You nah seh Death see no colour? You must be raging
that 'ma best-pal's-black' routine's fatally aging
Ma name's not Boab – am no a Zombie
Tho it's been long time since he deid
he's no the only Scottish Jamaican dread
Don't call me a Zombie – that cannae be right
Last time I checked back-a-yard jumbies are white.

Renaissance

Alice Bugg

His shoes were filled with dirty rainwater now, and his jacket was so wet that it clung to him like a heavy slice of wet fish. But, head down against the driving curtain of rain, he strode purposefully onwards. Nothing could dull his urgent sense of purpose. Now he knew, at last, where he had to go.

Something wasn't quite right. He stood back, frowned, tilted his head. His eyes flicked across to the right. And he realized. It was wee Alec. The ever present twinkle was missing from the otherwise glum face. With a swift squeeze and a careful, eloquent brushstroke he restored him to his usual appearance.

He heard the harsh clack-clacking of Nan's heels as she came briskly down the stone-flagged passageway from the cellar; the creak as she lifted the flap at the side of the bar counter; and felt her violet cachou-ed breath on the back of his bare neck.

'Aw, Sandy. That's braw. Is it finished, son?'

'Aye, that's me done with it. What do you think?'

She stood back, her hands clasped admiringly and smiled broadly at him: Nan, who had the eyes of an eagle, a brain like one of these new-fangled pocket calculators, a heart of gold and a tongue like a raw-hide whip. Nan, the unquestionable boss of the public bar. She had the burnished corn-yellow hair of a typical barmaid, but there the similarity stopped. Under the sleek and shining helmet of gold was the lined and plainish face of a late middle-aged woman whom you might see getting off any Glasgow bus, or in any Glasgow supermarket, buying a wee quarter of chopped pork for her tea.

But Nan ruled this bar – the public bar: this wee snug at the front of the ancient building which housed three separate bars. None of your fancy upholstered banquettes like upstairs, no carpet, no glinting brasses nor plastic flowers here. Just the plain wooden counter, worn smooth and warm with years of polishing, and simple wooden tables and chairs. A place for serious drinking.

And now, thanks to Nan, and to his talent, this bar was even more special. It had a mural. Along the back wall, behind the two round tables, he had painted a frieze of the regulars: Auld Shug, Wee Alec, Jim, Hector, Frank and Rab. All in their accustomed positions, with their usual drinks; painted in their dull, nicotine browns and wet Glasgow greys, under the cosy fug of the metal shaded, yellowed light-bulbs.

By the time Micky came down from the office to look at the finished painting, Auld Shug was sitting in the corner, nursing his Fowler's Wee Heavy and his whisky chaser; Wee Alec was standing, leaning his elbows up on the end of the bar, with his hauf'n'a hauf; and Jim, Hector, Frank and Rab were at their usual table, pints of heavy to hand.

'The boay's done a gran' joab therr, Micky. Much ur ye peyin' him furrit?'

'It's grand' said Micky, beaming (Micky was always beaming). 'McGinn'll be pleased – he'll gie him something.'

'Aye,' muttered wee Alec, barely moving his lips. 'That'll be right. Mean auld bastart'll gie ye fuck all!'

Wee Alec's prediction was incorrect, for once. McGinn had taken £20 from the till and handed it to him graciously; even almost-smiled at him. It was enough to pay two weeks rent on his damp and peeling bed-sit. Except he wasn't going to use it for that.

This money heralded the start of his career as a professional artist. This was just the beginning: he could see fame and fortune ahead of him and a lifetime full of lavish opening parties in novel exhibition spaces with moneyed patrons and gob-smacked critics fawning over him; he could see himself, wearing carefully paint-daubed casual gear, beer bottle in hand, surrounded by the adoring glitterati. Oh, yes. This was just the beginning.

So he blew the whole twenty quid at *Rico's* that night, buying drinks for all his art school mates, and anyone else who smiled at him. And thus it was he met Evelyn.

While he was still riding high on his cloud of optimism and Stella Artois, he realized that she had the most beautiful eyes he had ever seen; told her that she was the woman of his dreams; swept her off her feet, literally, and carried her out into the midnight streets. All the way back to his poky little room.

And that was the end of his dreams. For, on that very night, Sheila-May and Annie-Rose were conceived.

And so the last twenty years had passed in a blur of babies and nappies; dirty dishes, piles of washing, bills and DIY; and, of course, letters, parcels and postcodes: he'd worked first as a postman, and then, when he no longer had the stomach for the early mornings of foul weather and vicious dogs, as a sorter at the depot.

In the early days, as he walked his round, his mind would be full of ideas for paintings. He would refine and develop them as he went up and down the hollow closes. And, when he returned to their cramped little council house in the afternoon, he was primed and ready to start applying paint to canvas. But it never happened; not after the first few months, anyway. There was always a screaming baby to be changed, fed, soothed or supplied with some fresh air. There was always a household chore or some repair which was urgently required and which Evelyn couldn't manage to do.

Apparently, there wasn't much Evelyn *could* do in those days. The minute she heard his key in the door she would retire to bed, where she lay, white and exhausted, but still unable to sleep. And later, even when everything had been done, and the twins were both asleep at the same time, and Evelyn had re-appeared, slightly less white and drawn, all he was ready for was to slump in front of the television with a can of beer.

Over the years things got easier on the domestic front. But then again, with all the extra mouths to feed – at first just the two, then three, then four, then six – he had to do all the overtime that came his way. So now he didn't get home until late at night, just in time to go early to bed, in preparation for tomorrow's early shift.

Then, after ten years of learning to cope with her own children, Evelyn decided to train as a teacher. Once she'd qualified, she quickly landed a permanent job – which left her more stressed and bedraggled than ever. The extra money meant he could cut his overtime – but instead he had to hurry home to collect the children from school, feed them, help them with their homework and chase them off to bed. It had seemed to be a cycle of toil that would never end.

And then, last night, he had become aware that, at last, he had some free time. Time for himself. Sitting in the kitchen with a mug of coffee, he had suddenly realized how quiet it was. With the oldest three now away at University, Sarah-Lou studying in her room for her exams, Andrew and Fraser at football practice, and Evelyn snoring quietly in front of the television, he was effectively alone in the house. And free. The dishes were washed, the clean clothes had been folded and put away, and he'd even managed to wash the kitchen floor and clean the oven.

He'd felt something flicker deep inside him. Indigestion? Too much paprika in tonight's goulash? And then, with a growing sense of excitement he'd realized – it was his creative urge. It had returned, after all these years. He wanted to paint. He needed to paint. He *had* to paint. Now. Now. Right now.

He pulled open the back door, ran down the crazed path to the shed, almost dived inside and started pulling out the boxes which held all his old paints and brushes, his easel and his canvases. They were all there, everything he needed. He hurled old bicycles and garden tools, a spare tyre, some plant pots and boxes of goodness-knows-what out onto the scrubby grass, heedless of the crashes and thunks and shattering noises they made. With trembling hands he set up his easel. Positioned a medium-sized canvas on it. Grabbed his palette, squeezed out some still-useable paint. And froze, suddenly numb. The palette fell from his nerveless fingers and he stood for a while, listening to his slowing heart-beat. Waiting for it to stop altogether. Almost hoping it would.

The dog next door barked fiercely as he slammed the shed door shut behind him.

He lay in bed all night, curled into a tight little ball, trying to contain the hurt, to master the hole at the centre of his being. In the wee small hours, he realized that he couldn't. He unwound, and lay desolate, heart-broken, and silently weeping. He wept until the twirping and skraiking of the early birds reminded him that another day at the sorting office was due to start.

Slowly, he raised his head from the sodden pillow. He looked across at Evelyn, still peacefully deep in sleep, dreaming, no doubt, of times tables and spelling rules and the days when children hadn't answered back to their teachers. He reached out and touched her crumpled face. She stirred irritably, muttered, and turned away from him. He eased himself stiffly from the bed.

In the bathroom mirror he saw the face of a stranger – eyes pink and swollen, lines and wrinkles sharpened and deepened by his troubled night – framed by fast-greying hair which stuck out angrily. He threw down his razor, unused, left the bathroom and quickly put on his weekend clothes.

Then he left the house.

He walked, and walked, and walked. For hours and hours he walked. Standing, foot-weary, at the top of the Cathkin Braes, with the wind tearing at his hair, and stinging his eyes, he watched all the busy cars and buses and trains tearing across the dusty city. They seemed to be moving faster than usual. No time to stop. No time to think. Just keep moving. Just keep moving. And he found his feet carrying him fast downhill. Faster and faster. And suddenly, he knew where he was going.

Back to the pub. Back to Nan's pub. To see his mural. His last great *oeuvre*. Something told him that just seeing it again, just being in that pub, with his painting, would carry him back over the years. Back to those days when he had known he had greatness in him. When he had known where his future lay; what his life's work would be.

He took a bus to the city centre and then he walked. People passed him in a busy blur. He couldn't see their faces, couldn't see what they were thinking, became convinced that they weren't thinking. And that didn't matter. They were all just part of the scenery.

His feet no longer hurt, and he did not even realize that it had started to rain; that he was getting wetter and wetter, that his shoes were sodden and his jacket was sodden and that rain was dripping from the tip of his nose and the ends of his fingers.

And then he was there. And the door was no longer that dusty claret, beloved of these old pubs. But the step was familiarly worn down, and he felt like falling to his knees and kissing it. And he pushed the door open, and …
just

couldn't

take it all

in.

The room was vast: acres of space, dotted with aluminium stools and tables and there was lime-green, or was it pistachio, yes, it was pistachio, paint on the walls, and, somewhere at the back, a long way away, a huge, menacing, black slab of granite sat atop some bleached-out wood, and optics and glass shelves full of bottles glinted from behind, and he was aware of Robbie Williams' voice being piped through speakers, as he stood there. As he stood there, on his tired feet, dripping onto the polished laminate floor. And he could hardly breathe, hardly stand, could barely feel the floor beneath his feet, swayed and felt a hand at his elbow, a firm pressure, turning him, pushing him, towards the door. 'Come on. Out.' And he moved, unable to resist, unable to focus, or see, or think. And then a voice, a gruff voice, from the corner by the door: 'Let the lad alane. He's orright. Here, get 'im a brandy. Can you no' see 'e's jist wet? Here, take a seat, Sandy.'

And, as he sat down on the pistachio-cushioned window seat, he raised his head and found himself looking into the weaselly-wise eyes of wee Alec. Aye, wee Alec.

'Sit, lad. Sit there. Here's yer drink.'

He swigged back the proffered brandy, gasped as it hit the back of his throat, and then found himself able to breathe properly once again.

'Alec?' hoarsely, 'What've they done? My painting? My mural!'

'It's a new broom they've goat in here. Tried to get rid of me an a'. But I'm no a wan fur change. Och, dinnae dae that, son. Take yer heid oot yer hauns. That'll dae naebdy nae guid.'

'But, Alec. I'm done. I'm lost. I've painted nothing all these years. I came back to find myself, to remember where I started, where I was… who I am. I needed to see it again. To remind myself what I can do, what I'm capable of. To get me started again. I had to see it. And it's gone. This is the end.' And he groaned.

Wee Alec took another sip of his whisky. 'Naw, son'. He leaned closer over the table, lowered his voice, said with conviction, ''is is only ra be*ginn*in'.'

And, as he caught the twinkle in wee Alec's eye, he felt a tickle, somewhere deep inside and he suddenly found himself beginning to laugh. And he laughed, and laughed, and, as he laughed, he felt a warmth spread through him, starting from his gut, working its way up through his chest and down his arms, until his fingers began to itch and tingle. And he grasped wee Alec's hand firmly, squeezed it tight.

'Alec,' he roared, 'you're a bloody genius! A real pal. An inspiration!' Then lifted him from his seat in a huge bear-hug, set him back down on his feet, and ran out through the freshly-painted green door.

Wee Alec sat down again, took another sip of his whisky, and then the corners of his mouth lifted – just a wee bit.

Expecting

Julie Pallesen

For nine months, and no particular reason she can remember, she dresses up as pregnant. To begin with, all she has to do is to think that she is. Maybe drink too much water so she feels bloated. Slowly she gains a bit of weight. Not too much though, just enough for her breasts to feel heavier and her cheeks to go round. As the months go by, she wears bigger and bigger pillows on her stomach. She wears stockings under her trousers, fits the pillow under the stretchy nylon and makes sure that it is shaped so it looks right. It feels warm and safe. Pregnancy is her companion, she thinks. People treat her differently; they open doors for her, old men smile and think of times long past. Women envy her, she looks good pregnant, a natural pregnant. Proportionally it suits her very well and she is not a troubled or heavy walker; she glides easily, almost jumpy despite the big bump on her front.

Nine months and four days go by and something has to be born, she thinks. So this day in October, she sits on the steps outside the shopping galleries in town, a mild day, wearing jeans with a stretchy pouch for the belly and a blue cotton jumper showing off the round shape. She decides to give birth to an idea. She pulls her jumper over the belly and pulls the rounded pillow out of the stockings. With the idea in mind and a new face, a determined face that knows something, she leaves the pillow that is still warm from touching her stomach on the steps. As she walks, she holds on to the stretchy pouch of her jeans so they don't slide down.

Her face stays like that for a while, stays knowing of something and determined, but she does not know what to do with the idea. The idea is quiet. Too quiet. It does not ask her anything, does not keep her up at night, it is not wonderful and incredible. Maybe it does not belong to her, she begins to think. The idea is simply there and she doesn't know what to do with it.

Maybe she just has to wait, she figures. She stays in her flat most days. (She can't go back to work. She quit because she was expecting, she had told her supervisor sometime in her early pregnancy. Not that she misses work anyway). But she goes for walks at night. When she walks home, she has this ritual that when she gets to the middle of the bridge she has to stop and look down at the water. Depending on how wet the weather has been, the river changes. Sometimes it is brutal, rough and fast flowing. But she likes it that way. When it is noisy too, so she can't hear what she is saying, if she says anything, when she leans her head over the railing to get a full view, to take in as much blackbrown flow as possible.

The best place in her flat is in the bathroom a rectangle of perhaps three by four meters. There is the shower with the curtain missing, just the shower-curtain-pole hanging so you know where it used to be, or potentially could be. The bath is also gone. There is a toilet in the corner, just an average one, with an average flush. A mirror hangs on the rear wall, a mirror that stretches your image slightly. She spends a lot of time in the bathroom. Not to wash. It is a good place to think, or to not think too much about anything. In the bathroom you are excused. You don't have to explain, you are just going to the bathroom because everybody needs to go to the bathroom. Not that she would need an excuse with nobody around. From the shower you can see out. There are no curtains and clear glass. Not that there is much to see, she thinks. A deprived back lane with the odd rubbish and half deteriorated furniture that was never collected growing the opposite way of the grass that is never cut. The window is quite big, considering it is a bathroom. Possibly the room was converted from a normal room into a bathroom sometime. She would never have bothered getting curtains or blinds. And she doesn't really mind. If somebody would happen to walk by he or she might see a young woman showering. See her naked, pale skin and flat wet hair.

Time in her flat with the idea means a lot of time spent standing still and a lot of time lying about. Maybe she thinks about things too. But mostly she simply forgets herself in places. For example she will lie on the floor in the hall for no particular reason. She is a piece of leftover material, maybe something that could have been important. A nail lying around, waiting for someone to pick her up and bang her into place.

She has been for one of her night walks. On her way back to her flat she meets the man. She is walking along on the bridge, before the spot where she usually leans over the railing to look down at the river. The man is standing in her spot. He looks at her. His eyes are a sort of blue that that could be a mix between white cloud and blue sky. They are so blue that it doesn't look attractive. As if it isn't his eyes; they don't fit his face or his dark hair and by no means do they fit his unapproachable, awkwardly large body. He resembles a bear, with not quite controllable limbs, with arms that have large heavy hands that unintentionally knock things over with a force that scares people. Glasses fly across tables and doors slam so the walls shake. Hands that he mostly tries to keep out of trouble, buried deep in his pockets and long legs with feet that don't fit normal shoes. An odd ambiguity of a man. Out of scale and proportion. The world doesn't really want him to fit. And those unsuitable eyes. Those eyes that are not attractive, although they are. Eyes that truly see. Eyes that are not shy at all, that give a direct look and see through anything. You could not lie looking into his eyes. But you would not lie anyway, he is so big that there is nothing to lie about. At first he is looking at her, then he is looking at the river. (Where she would be able to get her shoulders over the railing, the whole of his upper body is over the edge.) Then he looks at her. She is a good distance from him, but he looks right at her. Those eyes. It is night and the river is black. (Sometimes it is black during the day too when it is raining.) There is nobody else on the bridge but her and the man. A man with too much of him, too much volume, too long in all directions and too much mass to be pulled down by gravity, so he moves slowly. Slowly he moves closer to her. He stops once he is an arm's length from her (his arm's length). He is not going to say anything, she can tell. Maybe that is why she gives him the idea. Like that, with her eyes she lets him have it. The eyes close, the big man's eyes, and he leaves. He leaves with the idea and his long white cane finding the streets, finding his way back to somewhere. She decides not to look at the river again. At least for a good while. She feels light and her legs are not just walking along; they are jumpy and energetic and can take her anywhere. The big man will know exactly what to do with the idea, she feels, and she thinks that maybe she should become pregnant again.

Why go to Glasgow?

Robin Burgess

Why go to Glasgow? Why not!?

Weather Report

Robin Burgess

I once went to Glasgow
and they told me it never rains but it pours
they even have words to describe the deluges and torrents and cascades
but when I went
it was sunny and warm.

What do I know…

Robin Burgess

What do I know
Of Glasgow?
… well I see the work of The Boys
At the glorious Kelvingrove Gallery
… it is wonderful
Also I see the work of the colourists –
… it is beautiful
I climb steep hills
And see distant horizons
Clear in the freshly washed air
And glistening sun
I see steep old roads
It is my first walk around
I am an explorer
I am not a Glaswegian
I am not a Norwegian
I am no 'egian' at all
I am just looking.

Flatmate

IJ Marcus

Do you know what I hate about motorways? Drivers. I hate drivers that cruise along in the middle lane for miles on end. The middle lane is for overtaking only, like the fast lane. Who do these idiots think they are? Are they not aware of the basic rules of motoring? I once rang up Jeremy Vine's Radio 2 show to participate in a heated discussion on the subject of middle-lane drivers. By the time I got through they had started talking about something else, namely whether mainstream non-organic underarm deodorants caused cancer or not, so I declined an invitation to comment. However, my failure to publicly condemn these mindless people has not detracted from my annoyance at their behaviour.

At a dinner party some time ago, I met a man who drove a canary yellow Ferrari Supercar in his spare time. On learning of his vulgar obsession, I took an immediate dislike to him. Buying such a car is an act of desperation, a sign that a person is insecure within himself. When asked about his motorway driving habits, he confessed to a love of the middle lane. How predictable! I thought to myself, as I tucked into a portion of rather over-sweet charlotte russe that sat on my plate. How predictable that a man of such little taste would prefer the middle lane. A mediocre man, attempting to appear flamboyant and glamorous with his ridiculous car, was thus exposed as the ignorant, inflexible human being he really was.

I could go on. But I shan't. Instead, I shall tell you a little about myself and my surroundings. My name is Andrew Mullen. I am twenty-eight years old. My current location is a courtyard behind a tenement building in Dennistoun, Glasgow. I can hear the afternoon traffic going past, being as I am near to a major local thoroughfare, Alexandra Parade. I often think about going for a walk in the nearby Alexandra Park, within which can be found the first ever fountain to be made entirely from iron. A pioneering fountain of the Victorian age, fallen into disrepair. My respect for Glasgow City Council wanes every time I think about that fountain. Where is their sense of civic dignity, of municipal integrity? If they can't even maintain one fountain it's no wonder the stabbing statistics are through the roof.

Dennistoun is surrounded by depressing, crime-ridden mini towns. Young men walk about in sub-zero temperatures in nothing but white football shirts and tracksuit bottoms, sneering at you as you drive past. Down the Cumbernauld Road you drive, down the Dalmarnock Road. To Cambuslang you go, Shettleston, Ruchazie, Springburn and Easterhouse. Murder and gay rape in the parks, dirty drugs running through the veins of babies.

I'm not a Glaswegian myself. Born and raised Great Yarmouth boy. The mobile phone company I was working for reassigned me to the Glasgow office seven years ago, but the Scots have never made me feel welcome in this city. They are a remarkably unfriendly people, who seem to think urinating on the stairwells of apartment buildings is appropriate social behaviour. It is quite normal for a glued-up Celtic fan to approach you in the street and attempt to put you in a headlock for no apparent reason. While thuggish youths break into cars and wrench the steering-wheel locks off with crowbars, the local residents walk past oblivious, too drunk to care. The hairdresser will sell you a bag of drugs with your cut and blow-dry, and when the drains overflow, sewage spills onto the pavement. It doesn't get cleaned up for days on end.

When I first moved here, I took a one bedroom flat on the south side of the city. Nice enough I suppose, though I was the only one in the building who spoke English as a first language, which really got on my wick after a while. About six months in, a group of young Scottish men moved in above me, which I thought would be an improvement to the situation. How wrong I was. There were about six of them, and they took the two flats in the building that had been uninhabited for months. The day they moved in they had an enormous party that kept me up all night. Thinking that the anti-social noise levels and vomiting out the window could be justified by the fact that it was probably a house-warming party, I let it slip. However, this behaviour continued unabated for weeks on end. When I went up to complain, they laughed in my face and told me to get a life. Then the big house across the road got burgled by a gang. The criminals shot the owner of the house dead in front of his wife and kids before running off with a huge lump of cash. Why that man had so much cash in his house I don't know. What I do know is that it was a Pakistani gang. Well I don't know that for sure, but 95% of the people on the

South Side are from Pakistan, so it's very likely.

At the present moment, total darkness surrounds me. My nose is continually affronted by the revolting smells of rotting food and used female sanitary products. Maggots and rats are my only companions, save for the occasional resident from the tenement block. They come down to dispose of their rubbish in the metal bins in the courtyard. They don't talk to me, but I don't care. None of them would be worth speaking to anyway. They have all been nothing but rude to me.

I didn't have a lot of friends in Glasgow when I first moved here, so I made an extra effort to make some. I knocked on my neighbour's doors, introduced myself by my first name and insisted that if they ever needed any sugar, they knew where to come. They all looked at me as if I was an illegal sex worker, which I'm not.

It has been difficult. All I wanted was to feel at home here. After all, there's little else to console a stranger to the west coast of Scotland, with its freezing winters and continual rain. But if you're not Scottish, the Scottish hate you. They won't give you the time of day in the street. I know that my English accent is off-putting for them and yes, I know about the centuries of oppression at the hands of the English, but really, I think they should just accept their inferior status and learn to live with it. England was, is and always will be the stronger, more prosperous nation, with better weather and fewer drug problems. Why should I feel ashamed of where I'm from?

Despite the hostility I was confronted with, I decided to battle on. In order to facilitate my assimilation, I started to frequent my local pub, the Lea Rig. It was an unsuccessful venture. In the front bar, middle-aged men sat on their own, not speaking to anybody, while unattractive women sat in the lounge area around the back. You can only nurse your pint in front of gyrating pop stars on the TV for so long before you start to feel worse than when you came in.

Nobody does anything in this city, that's what I don't like. They make up reasons why they can't go out and work, like obesity, or depression, or the fact that they've got a child, and then go pleading to the government for benefits. There are 60,000 people in Glasgow on benefits, more than any other UK city. And I bet at least half of them are committing benefit fraud. And then, even if they do go out and work during the week, they get absolutely obliterated all weekend on drink and drugs. This is not fun-loving hedonism; it's a collective, childish denial of the realities of life.

Take my flatmate Chris for example. He's a twenty-seven year old accountant, who's originally from East Kilbride, one of the nicer parts of Glasgow. I found him through the 'Flatmate Wanted' section of a classifieds website. He's a nice enough guy, and he wasn't too bad as a flatmate, but he was lazy. He would smoke in the house even though the landlord explicitly forbade it, because he couldn't be bothered to go outside. After cooking, he would leave his dishes to fester for a good day before finally giving them a cursory clean. I once found a dead fly attached to one of the spoons in the drawer. In the drawer! When he brushed his teeth he would leave flecks of toothpaste on the bathroom mirror, never bothering to clean them off. He ignored the fact that the curtain was not properly attached to the curtain rail at one end for over three weeks. In the end I had to fix it myself. I could never concentrate on a book because the TV or the radio was always on. Background noise distracts me. These things may seem petty, but they add up, I can tell you. In the long run, they can have a very negative effect on your quality of life.

In protest, I started doing the chores just after he went to bed during the week, stomping around so that I would keep him awake. One morning, he said he was convinced we were being burgled at one am, but I assured him it was just me taking the rubbish out. Oh right, was all he said. When I had had enough of his tardy bill paying, I took to speaking to him about bills the minute he got home from work. You have yet to make the transfer into my account for the energy bill, I would say, as he slumped down, exhausted, on the sofa. I don't care if you've been busy, I'd say. I don't care that it slipped your mind. He told me once I was like his mother, only his mother didn't nag him as much. I didn't rise to the bait.

Personally, I don't think we ever saw eye to eye. Not really. In an attempt to improve matters in our flat I took to writing little reminders on post it notes. I put them absolutely everywhere, so there's no way he couldn't have seen them, but he never did any of the things I suggested. He didn't take the bin out, he didn't defrost the freezer, he didn't clean the oven, he rarely bought the milk. The list goes on.

There were tensions, but we still got on. It did hurt when he didn't turn up to my birthday drinks year after year, but I forgave him. When he laughed at my keen appreciation of Masterchef, I kept quiet. It's true we were different politically, sexually, and intellectually, seeing as he was a repressed homosexual with a limited worldview, but I thought we were buddies. So why? Why did he feel the need to knock me out by throwing the iron at my head? And what drove him to cut my head off with the bread knife once I was rendered unconscious? Maybe he thought I was cramping his style when I came out with him and all his friends? Maybe he thought I should have made my own friends? I just don't know.

So now here I am, in the courtyard round the back. A human head in a bin bag. It's amazing when you think about it, the way my life has changed. One minute, I'm making a cup of tea, the next I've been decapitated. I thought that when your head was severed from your body you died pretty much instantaneously, but for some reason I'm still perfectly cognisant. This has turned out to be quite annoying. For example, Chris owed me £80 for the electricity bill at the time of my beheading, but now there is no way I can get that money back. The other annoying thing is that I've got no idea where the rest of my body is. It could be anywhere. Maybe Chris made lasagne with the meat and served it up to one of his girlfriends? Maybe he chopped me up, put me in individual jiffy bags and stored me in the freezer? I hope he did put me in the freezer, because at least then he'll have had to chuck out those out of date fish fingers and microwave meals to make room.

The bin bag I'm in was cursorily thrown into one of several metal dustbins seven days ago. All the bins are now full to the brim, but the bin men still haven't been round to collect the rubbish. Isn't that astounding? I was tempted to write a letter of complaint to the council, I really was.

Since I've been dead, Chris has been having sex constantly. I know this because the flat is on the first floor and he leaves his bedroom window open. This continual love-making must be a gratifying indulgence on his part, seeing as I strictly forbade him from having sex in the flat unless I was out. Now that I have permanently left the building he can fuck as much, and as loudly, as he likes. He dumped his girlfriend a couple of months ago, so this one must be a new girl. I bet he met her through the 'Casual Encounters' section of a classifieds website.

'slim, solvent, non white ,your pics,,,lives in rivur been illegimitely single since 1977 is millenaire gets ,,,mines pic non chinese nonblack man slim very black suntanned turban on dick hair pubes tied in ponytail dumbass thick man robert james sherry brown rich man skint man tiny dick nonbmw driver non large penile owner seeks wife ukkraine woman who no speak lingo for longterm no moron take a look in mirror before you say i am a fat ugly dick-head useless cunting arselicking bi faggot married nonsingle fuckwit thanks'. That's the sort of thing that gets written in that section. You've really got to sort the wheat from the chaff on those sorts of sites. You get a lot of weirdos.

Chris isn't a weirdo. He's actually quite ordinary. He's a balanced, well-adjusted young man with a good income and a healthy social life. Even when he was about to kill me, his mind was clear and his reasoning was sound. As I poured the boiling water onto the teabag, he called to me from across the open plan kitchen and living area. Brandishing the iron high above him, he spoke in a measured, calm voice. 'I've never killed before', he said, 'but then, I've never met anyone like you'.

James Leo McAskill

'Christ of St John of the Cross' is unveiled to the people of Glasgow

How can it divine us? In love
with love's division or our sunken heads
coarseness. A codex of unmetered

faith. And what of our scrutiny,
retching over the tonnage of a neo-classical sky,
and of the fishermen, below a different

black-drop cross, working in pastel silence. Who,
cropped around the sermon, asks -
how can *this* body move us?

An altarpiece beyond the altar form.
Buying piety for a halfpenny, decoding
These muscles taught from sunshine

And hair curled metaphors
that seek no answers, lest they would be bold,
or more a picture than the faith requires.

I fear to take the leap into the sacrament
so hold the vigil silent and alone.
A painting is as good as a headstone.

What I Wouldn't Say

extract from a novel

Paul Deaton

I wasn't eating.

Or what I was eating was the dry bone meal of foods, sawdust really – Ready Brek in the morning, Ready Brek in the evening, reaching for it immediately, when I got in.

Inevitably I was losing weight.

I had this odd idea that to eat properly was to agree to everything, to agree to life. To consume one's nutritional share was like shaking hands with someone you didn't like; sort of like your parents forced you to do, for the benefit of family propriety. Someone turns up, a friend of theirs and the family puts on this false face and you go along with your shared role. The role the family has created, that somehow you don't know this compels your response, you play up to it unconsciously but it isn't at all what you feel, you do it only to make them, your parents, feel good. You don't let them down but it is all a huge front, and you know this but do it anyway, as though the only time everyone came together was if an outsider was present in the family and then this automatic response kicks in, collectively, that made us all seem so well, so chipper, so altogether and harmonious. But a front is all it is and what hurts most is you do it anyway, that you are forced or have forced yourself to play your part in the facade, their facade.

There is no other way of acting in this family, for it isn't a family but a totalitarian system, a regime, and you are trapped, daily sinking, daily fighting for your life, and all the while being called upon to maintain the facade, the habits of a vague decorum.

And the truth, the sordid truth, was I knew we were gone to rot and everything was sick. And this was our lie. The lie of our family. One of them.

This is the past but it followed me like an expert assassin. And I didn't want to agree, be always so nice for my parents and my parents' family friends. How could I agree?

I didn't want to shake life's hand. I wanted to push life away, push everything away; slump down with my head on the table. Sleep. I longed for a deep sleep, annihilating. The sleep of death? Is this what I longed for?

A sleep where everything is forgotten? Where your own life is forgotten?

'But that is death,' the short plump psychiatrist had smugly told me.

Eating Ready Brek was my minimal compromise.

If I ate properly I thought I might as well live how everyone else lives, greedily devouring more than their share. Eat and consume, that is how I saw life going on around me; everybody blindly chomping in huge carnivorous mouthfuls; not just food; wading in a river of material gluttony, insatiable. People like piranhas, gnashing their jaws and putting on the dressed front of a desirable life.

But I was resistant; a small act but a necessary one, a private rebellion. I wanted to hold back on my consumption. I did it with food. It occurred to me in my ailing state, my thawing thinness, my starvation, that I might have stumbled on a psychological theory of anorexia. My struggle was no different: was at root an inability to say '*Yes*'. Food. An anger turned inside. And herein lies the introvert's resistance.

I'd line the red cereal boxes up in the cupboard. It hadn't occurred to me I was buying one a day and even though I was doing my best to empty them as quickly as possible (it was all I ate when I got in of an evening, it had become the first thing I did) I couldn't keep up with my purchases.

I had five boxes in a line, three of which were opened and in a varying state of emptiness. I held them up and shook them before I made my choice, listened for the dull mealy noise to muffle inside. There were empty boxes strewn on the linoleum floor: one by the cupboard, three in the top of the bin, two at its side and then several, in a neat row, under the window where I preferred to place them, when I was seeing things in a more orderly way. That said when I looked at them I wanted to break up the order of that row. If the TV ads were anything to go by now I wasn't orange sealed, body aureoled; I was positively irradiated.

What's more, I knew I was lactose intolerant, yet I was buying full cream milk. It was another sort of concession. I allowed myself full cream milk thinking that this would make up for my dietary deficiencies, again the power of advertising. The dull phrases beamed up in my mind, 'lotta bottle', as did the bald man's cheesy grin and his staggering electric milk cart. More neurons fired from our family's narcotic watching of TV.

But I was reaping the costs. My skin felt like it was crawling with larvae and the oats were turning my insides out. My face was coming out in red heat blotches, beetroot flushes, and my tongue felt like a trapped wet toad. It was difficult to swallow yet I kept eating my Polyfilla paste from my one china bowl my mum had bought me when I went to uni; one of a set of three: dinner plate, bowl, starter dish. I think she got them from a discount store like Woolworths or maybe we even got them from collecting stickers on the back of cereal boxes. We did things like that when I was growing up; me and my sister ended up collecting all manner of useless crap.

But what I do remember is that in that way of cheap items, they weren't very pleasing to look at and weren't very practical either. The bowl, for instance, had quite a wide rim so that the concave bit in the middle was quite small, the size of a small half grapefruit or large orange. It really would only take a few mouthfuls of cereal, and if I wasn't careful I was always slopping milk over the sides. So when I was eating I stayed near the Ready Brek boxes because I had to keep refilling it. The plates, too, suffered from the same issue, an over wide rim which made the plate part quite small. These three plates really annoyed me but it was as though I was stuck with them because my mum had given them to me. It didn't occur to me to ditch them; I kind of looked after them even though I hated them. And another thing, they were indestructible. Those plates really annoyed me. I had thought of throwing them out from my high windows like a Frisbee into the yard far below me, watching them bend and sail away. This would have given me great pleasure and it may have changed things, but I didn't; like a lot of things, I left it at an imaginary thought. They probably wouldn't break up and would lie there unmoved on the ground, eyeing me, in their discarded white loneliness, each time I came to the window. It would get to the point that I wouldn't even be able to come to the window and look out; knowing they were down there in that derelict stone gravel yard, their pearly whiteness watching for me. Resenting me.

I'd kept the plates but had dropped uni and was dropping everything else they had ever given me. The funny thing was when I was at uni I didn't know I would drop it. I had spent one afternoon talking to a casual friend; Deborah, I think her name was.

She was one of those tall solid girls (not overweight), as large if not larger than most tall men; long limbs, large hands, tall torso, hunched shoulders like an ox, and a boxer's thick heavy jaw, the sort of scale that when you see them walking you expect them to be male, a person like a semi-mature tree that permits you only to walk widely around them, give them berth and then when you realise they are female it comes as a surprise. She stood out.

She had wandered over to me. I couldn't help myself wondering about the challenges she would present in bed, how you would get at her, and somehow, for no reason, she started telling me, in the mid afternoon quiet of the deserted bar area, how unhappy she was, which was odd because I thought she was one of the sorted ones.

She had a gravelly voice that seemed to match the size of her frame. Then she let out this really very long sigh like a hovercraft deflating and went for it, but all very calmly.

'I'm not enjoying the course, are you?' She never waited for a reply but went on. 'It's too theoretical; what is it really going to give me? I'm fed up where I'm living and the people in my halls … do you like the people in your halls?'

I thought about who was in my halls and how many of them I really hadn't got to know. There was Angus, who I drank with. And the two girls who went about together like a couple of magpies. But the rest. All ten of them. What of them? Angus was always dreaming of his brunette girlfriend from back home who hadn't yet visited him. She's got great legs and long hair he often said, which was as much as I ever got to know about her; that and that he longed for them to back in their rightful place, wrapped tightly around him.

'My last mark was quite poor,' Deborah went on 'and I had worked well for it. Being a dumb passive student is getting to me; maybe I shouldn't be here right now doing this. Who in the world will want a philosophy major anyway?' It all started to build into a landslide like her sigh and I wondered where this all came from and why in fact she was telling me.

When I had seen her around campus she was always walking slowly, so slowly that I assumed she must know where it was she wanted to get to. I figured you wouldn't walk slowly and not know where you were going. Her speech was slow too and I couldn't figure how someone who talked slow and probably thought slow careful thoughts could have stumbled into this cul-de-sac. But I guessed, as she stared out across the bar area, she wasn't after my answers.

Anyway, I listened thoughtfully and tried to reassure her that it would all work out. I surprised myself and came up with a list of the positives: 'there were worse places to be, it is only the second term, get to the end of the year and you'll feel different' I said. I could have thought of more. I even said 'you're one of the more solid ones', which I realised was a dumb thing to say, a giveaway, as if this could help her, but the thought of her size was stuck in my mind. I'm very slight, you, and my life has never felt heavier than a feather. But it didn't matter, she was still somewhere way across the other side of the bar.

Well, to cut the story short, it was the very next day, after our discussion that I went to see my course tutor and said that I was leaving this charade and nothing could change my mind. John Samuels. I liked him. He was a stoic.

A City Story

Mohamed Rokadiya

When, late on that musty afternoon, you asked
'How is it you'll remember me?' I couldn't
say what poison, what potion it was that led
back to Park Road, to the riot of voice outside
Sonny's (pricking the languid ears inside).
And you too, heard us. Idle streetlights set the dark
stage for our show – my burning cigarette breathed
its last – and we separated hastily as paper
in a spine-broken book. There will be no more,
no encore; no. Glasgow, I have outgrown you
as a stem does its seed. I have drowned in this
journey, let the Clyde heave away that story.
Here's my last: 'How is it I'll remember you?'

The Dandelion Woman

Stephanie Brown

Once upon a time, I lived among the detritus of the generations in an elegantly dilapidated flat in St Petersburg, where an ancient grandfather clock had stood proudly among the roses on the wallpaper for many years. Because I had never known my grandfather, and thought that Grandfather Clock was a name, I sometimes imagined the clock was really my grandfather. I pictured his cupboard popping open one day as he chimed the hour like an oven to reveal my mother inside as a fresh and squirming babe, cooked and ready. Like a sentinel, he watched over us all; Mother as she made delicious concoctions in the kitchen, Father as he made serious faces at the newspaper, and me as I whirled from room to room like a tiny dervish, in pursuit of imaginary foes.

Once upon a time I was bundled into the car at night without a word. I was taken away from the comforting click and whirr of my old friend to a place whose furniture is all plastic and has no soul. Now I stand on a high tower and watch the clouds forever burst over the city of Glasgow, and feel as though I am being punished for some obscure and momentary crime. The crime of being from the old Eastern Bloc, maybe. The crime of being daughter to my Father. But sure enough, time here will wash away our Eastern ways. Time enough and I'm sure I too will love sausage rolls, pints of Tennents, and the fake-tanned glamorama of the televised talent show. So too will our friends the Libyans, the Congolese, the Sri Lankans and the Iraqis; swept up together like the scurf of the world. Here, they sniff and spit and look at us sideways when we walk by. No one realises that we are all decent people. We don't belong here. No one belongs here, and yet everyone does.

Since I have been here I have grown and I have changed, but I still hope that we'll return home some day, no matter how impossible father says this is. I still think of old Grandfather Clock who marks the time for someone else, or maybe lies sadly in the corner with his moustaches drooping, gathering dust on the other side of the world.

Here in Glasgow I sit on the balcony of our high rise flat, listening to junkies scream at each other on the ground below. I recognise them because junkies look like junkies wherever you go in the world and speak the same language of the living dead. They howl incoherently on the ground below my feet like hungry wolves. At night I dream of them climbing the sides of this tower, creeping in the balcony and surrounding me with their hands held out, coming to suffocate me with their nasal cries of 'scuzemepalscuzemepalscuzemepal.' Sometimes I feel the tower move with the wind, but I'm safer up here than I am down there.

When I get bored of the balcony, I sometimes go and sit on the landing. The atmosphere of inside is too claustrophobic, with all three of us in such a small space; father continuously smoking and mother continually hatching useless plans to make money, the television droning on.

One day an old woman comes struggling up the stairs with a cargo of shopping as I sit on the landing reading my book. She is red and sweating, and moves with a particular rolling motion of the hips with her tongue out to one side. She is wearing a fleece adorned with a pack of wolves in wintertime, and her hair sticks straight up from her head in all directions like the puff of a dandelion. Just as she reaches me, her bags all seem to burst at the same time and her tins of ravioli go flailing down the stairs.

'Ah, sudas!' she shouts, and I run to catch them before they escape. I return with them, and pick up the chicken that's landed at her feet.

'Thank you, sweetie,' she says gratefully, clutching for the chicken.

'It's ok, I'll help you carry them,' I say, and return a shy smile to her various clucking noises of thanks.

'Where are you from?' I ask as we reach her door.

'Lithuania, but I lived in Siberia for many years... near the Road of Bones at Oymyakon...' she says, trailing off into the kitchen. I stand in her hallway awkwardly, holding the chicken. Her flat is dark and smells of animal. A stuffed bird looks back at me from the afterlife on the sideboard. I gingerly place the chicken corpse next to it and begin to tiptoe out, while the woman hums tunelessly in the next room. Returning down the stairs, a geography lesson returns to me; Oymyakon: the coldest inhabited place on Earth.

Later that same night I notice the old lady ambling across the playground below our balcony (I recognise her lupine fleece), past some men who sit on the swings drinking Bucky. One of them shouts something at the lady, but this is not unusual here. What is unusual is that a fat raven strides up at this very moment and pecks at his trouser leg, making him spring up onto the seat of the swing. He flails a leg at it, but the bird merely cocks its head and lets out a threatening caw. His friends are laughing until another fat raven attacks the bald head of one, and yet another emerges comically from behind a bin like a mafia don. I'm laughing with glee at this unexpected Hitchcock scene, when suddenly the birds flap upwards as one and circle in an arc that gets wider until it disperses into the evening sky. All the while the old woman continues on her solitary path, heading with the determination of the undefeated to god knows where.

I don't understand the boys here. In the stairwell they surround me with sarcastic wolf-whistles and hoots and I don't understand why, if I am so repulsive, they have to come so close I can smell their cigarettes and cheese and onion crisps. I am not afraid of them: I carry a kitchen knife in these unfashionable jeans. I am not afraid of them, but they don't know this, so they come to surround me anyway.

'Woot woo,' one of them says, as if they were words. The others snicker behind him like hyenas propped up absurdly on back legs. They are hardly even older than me, but they're just enough older. Suddenly, I am sick of it all and don't even stop the words from hissing forth;

'Piss off.' This seems to greatly amuse them.

'Pees oaf, pees oaf,' they enjoy parroting, and block the stairs so I can't get past. Usually I would absorb their insults with saintly passivity, showing no emotion as I rushed to get past, and my silence would be like a shield that could not be penetrated. There is no fun in torturing a mannequin. I should have understood my Mother's advice to 'ignore them,' which was never about moral superiority, always about self-preservation. Now they bear down on me from above, really like animals, and I realise that this was what they wanted the whole time; the fight back, to see what snarling life in me was left. I take out my kitchen knife, which I now realise is pathetically blunt, and the leader is coming closer and I find myself backed into the wall, and he goes for his zipper and I think I don't know how I will live if I have to remember this, and my little knife falls and tinkles on the ground and nobody even notices it, it was such an impossible defence… And into this eternal moment of the about-to-happen snuffles and shuffles my dandelion-headed saviour, who arrives on the landing with a great wheezing and fuss to smile blithely at everyone;

'Hello boys… and girl,' she says, as they all look at her blankly, suddenly with the attitude of the innocent teenage boy.

'Hello Mrs,' one mumbles reverentially.

'Oh boys, you don't think you could help me carry my shopping, could you? I had to leave half of it down the stairs; I'm worried someone's going to lift it.' They mumble their assent and lope off to retrieve the shopping. Ms Dandelion shuffles on, and I slide my way up the wall, almost in disbelief to have been set free.

'Anya,' a knowing singsong voice calls from somewhere above my head, 'you dropped your knife… Come up later and I'll give you some pie.'

I sit at the door after this has happened, peering through the letterbox to make sure they have gone, but after several hours they don't come down from Ms Dandelion's. I decide I must have missed them, or they have gone into a flat upstairs, and feel it's safe to go and get some pie.

A rich smell beckons me up the stairs and I breathe it in gratefully, already imagining the pie in my stomach. I knock and there's no answer, so I push the door open gently and call 'Hello…' but silence reigns in Ms Dandelion's flat. The bird on the sideboard looks at me in fear, frozen in the attitude of death. I step onto the reeling psychedelic wonderland that is the carpet and feel my way along woodchip walls. 'Hello?' I call again, salivating for the pie. I let my nose lead me into the kitchen where sits the most luscious looking pie I have ever seen, freshly baked and steaming, garnished with two pastry leaves. It has been so long since I had a proper meal, I think, and I find myself gravitating, levitating towards the pie, hallucinating its crust and meat… But it occurs to me that I should not dig my fist into the pie and should wait for Ms Dandelion to offer me a slice. I turn away from it, breaking its spell, and go into the living room instead.

…There I find such a scene of horror it's impossible to comprehend. The boy sits with his zipper undone, propped up like a mannequin on a Queen Anne chair, eyes wide as the stuffed bird's and face frozen in that same attitude of fear, chest cracked open and a gaping hole there exposing a missing heart and parts like machinery, like… clockwork. I stand there mouth open until a loud caw makes me grip the carpet like a scared cat and I look up to see a huge raven perched on the edge of the balcony, looking at me, at us, with head to one side. It is then with a sickening lurch of the stomach that I notice the black feathers all around the room and the bird shit that plasters the floor. At the same time my head reels to think of the pie, the pie, and I retch and have to grab the wall. It's then that I notice the note that has fallen off the living room door;

'For Anya,' it says, 'Grandfather Clock is thinking of you. He waits for you in the halls of Sadovaya Street where he counts the minutes till your return. He wants you to know that the cats and the ghosts all wait for you and will always wait for you to come home. He wants you to be safe so you are welcome to this pie.'

Then I think of the woman from Oymyakon and know that Baba Yaga has followed me here, through the storybooks, through all these years. And just then a gust enters from the balcony and gathers the feathers and scatters them lightly into the wind like the puff of a dandelion, like the fragments of a dream dissolving.

The War on Terror

Ruth Dunster

This is the amazing true story of Amy Pershing, the insignificant mouse. It's amazing only because it happened, and it changed the world for her.

She was born on the night of a terrorist bombing which brought down an air liner, and the TV screens of her first day on earth replayed constantly a loop of images of smoking tangled wreckage that had fallen from the sky. A couple of hundred people were wiped off the earth in that event, that night.

Her parents tried to divert all conversations away from the event, to shield her from her terrible association with the day, but as the years passed, anniversary documentaries and over-zealous fact-finders reminded her often that she was born into a world of terror.

It came to light that the terrorists had aimed for a catastrophe of greater magnitude, planning the bombed aircraft to descend onto the city of her birth. Apparently (a source of satisfaction to the enemies of terror), the bombers, while setting the bomb's timing mechanism, had plotted out the straight timeline of the airliner's flight path without taking into account the curvature of the round earth. And so the liner was brought down in decimated fragments not onto the city where a child was being born, but instead onto a village fifteen minutes short of the intended destination of the terror.

This strangely fated escape haunted Amy as she grew through adolescence into her young adulthood. She engaged in not unusual goals for a person from her background – romance, career, an interest in art – but somehow held back by a lurking insecurity. By the time the twenty-fifth anniversary documentary was being made, Amy had become a quiet and inconspicuous visitor to the local psychiatric hospital, where a therapist made things considerably worse by exhorting her to face her fear and have some courage. People, apparently, died every day and the world somehow went on. The fear at this thought – of universal constant ongoing death – grew bigger and deeper, until it seeped into the earth and sky to turn her world into a blood-filtered environment of unmitigated terror. Amy began to fear going out of doors. Each time a plane flew overhead, she looked up in alarm and breathed a sigh of silent thanks to God when the engine noise receded into the distance. She began to pray, obsessively, for an endless list of places, people, cities, nations, ethnic groups, where terror threatened innocent lives. The daily news bulletins became an update for her never-ending concern. She stepped up her attendance at her local church, hoping to add her devotions to a tide of spiritual progress against hatred and terror.

Before long she had quit her job, too scared to face the day: quit going to the cinema (too likely a bomb target); quit getting on trains; planes – impossible. A walk down the shopping streets of the city revealed to her only the faces of people who shared her misery, or laughed and shouted in small clusters in a bid to shut out the fear. Eventually, the safe haven of her quiet semi became a place of terror too, as she began to hallucinate the smell of burning, and she would run out into the garden in barely concealed terror.

I'm beat, she said to the psychiatrist. He had no answers, beyond ever higher doses of medication and weekly chats which seemed somehow to make things worse.

I'm beat, she said to the pastor of her church. His answer was to pray more – which, of course, she did, in terror.

She looked up at the sky one barren frosty day. I'm beat, you know. There was no answer.

The only safe place was the big, run-down neglected garden – the birds sang, the sky, a panorama of shades of blue with pageants of clouds bringing greys and silvers across in constant change. The quiet there was wonderful. In a rotting old wooden shed she found a garden fork and spade. She began to dig the garden. While the birds sang and flitted around her, there was no need to pray. The rhythm of the fork and spade in turning over soil seemed a better silent prayer. She unearthed worms and beetles, and as she grew to recognise their varieties and their habits, the way they burrowed and scuttled to safety, she began to like them, to find them interesting. To the left, her elderly neighbour occasionally came out to put washing on the line or smoke a pipe and look out on the hills. To her right, teenagers wandered in and out of the deserted ruins of an old house. She hated the incursion into her world – hated the way they must be looking at her, wondering why a young woman did nothing, even on rainy days, but dig away at a big overgrown end-terrace garden. The rainy days, in fact, were best. The earth had a softness, moist and pliable; the flowers she had begun to plant soaked up suppleness from the wet ground. People did not come out to look at her on rainy days.

It was a long-sunned July day. She was tired, and stopped to lean on her spade, looking around at the wild expanse of weeds around her. I'll never do it, she thought. *This garden is too big for me.*

She stood, while birds were gliding high and silent in the sky above her and the sun played slow motion turning round the shadows. It was very still.

She thought of the old widowed man in the house on the left. She thought of the teenagers smoking fly cigarettes in the ruined house to the right. *The left is the past,* she thought. The right is the future. I'm standing here in the middle, here, now, in this moment. The silence kept its vigil of the sunshine and the soil. I'm standing here, she thought. She looked across to her left, across the yards of untouched deep rooted weeds. She looked to the right, across more of the same.

Nobody said to her, *you're safe.* Nobody could.

She made the decision to look ahead, not right, not left, and dig the space in front of her.

It was maybe five years later, long after the garden had become a landscaped place of pride to her, with its well kept lawns and beautifully wild plantings of sturdy buddleia, subtle alstromeria, dianthus, lavatera, sweet pea, geranium, standard rose, clematis… the wrought iron bench in the sunniest part overlooking the pond with its grasses and water lilies; the flowers all around that pond.

She had sat for morning coffee on the bench beside the pond, and made a shopping list. She was walking round the shops, and noticing how sunlight makes people smile.

She came home and made the dinner.

Oh, you won't want to watch the TV, her boyfriend said as he poured their mugs of tea. It's a big feature on the new evidence about the bombing.

No, I don't, I've seen it all before, she answered over her shoulder. They'll never get to the bottom of that, it's all too long ago. You watch it if you want though. It's just a different place and a different time. I want to get that painting of these flowers finished before they start to wilt.

The Lonesome Death of Brian Connolly

Richie McCaffery

There were the dragging,
delving weeks afterwards.
Plugged into machines
like a smashed up Strat
shoved through a Marshall stack.

But the last great gig
was falling backwards
down the stairs, pissed,
as if letting go into
the needy arms of the crowd

to surf on laurelled lyric
or bubble-gum adulation.
His heart rattling
like the Glasgow Subway shuttle
between Hillhead and Kelvinbridge.

Riding twenty years
with the same expired ticket.

Homecoming

for Edwin Morgan

Richie McCaffery

By the time I got home from a cul-de-sac job,
the makar on high had been cremated in Glasgow.

That evening, poet-friends boasted sightings of him,
Canedolian rara avis, most lyrical starling.

I have a memory of taking tea at Clarence Court
and the afternoon sun the brightest I'd seen.

As we talked of Veronica Forrest-Thomson
I felt my dead grandfather growing jealous.

The sun seethed when Eddie spoke, the light
of a mothership glaring between high tenements.

PEOPLE ALWAYS WALK PAST. NO ONE STOPS, NOT EVEN FOR A PHOTO.
NOT THIS AGAIN!
DAY AFTER DAY, STUCK ON A HORSE ON A PODIUM.
AT LEAST YOU'RE NOT THE HORSE!
EVEN THE PIGEONS GET MORE ATTENTION THAN ME!
DON'T YOU DARE!
I HATE MY LIFE.
YOU WERE PURE AFF YER FACE LAST NIGHT!
THAT'S NO WIT YER MAW WAS SAYING LAST NIGHT!

AM GONNA BATTER YOU!
WAIT! LOOK! TRAFFIC CONES!
YOU HINKIN WIT AM HINKIN?
AYE!
QUALITY!

YALDEE!
HA! PURE BEAST, MAN!
ERRAPOLIS!
C'MON BANKSY, GET DOWN.
TRAFFIC CONES WEEKLY
THE SKINNY
HAVE WE CONE MAD?
DUKE OF SWELLINTON
CHECK IT OOT. IT'S THAT MAD STATUE.
TAKE MY PICTURE WITH THE STATUE
SACRE BLEU!
SAY CHEESE!
UHMAZIN'!
OH-EM-GEE!
BEN STOP FEEDING THOSE STUPID PIGEONS AND COME SEE THIS BRILLIANT STATUE!
K.B

The Ballad of Catastrophe Jane and Hawaiian Dave

Frankie Gault

See me, see when ah go intae work on Monday, see Benny Boyle, ahm gonny fuckin kill him. How could ah be so stupid tae get roped intae this circus. Haud on a minnit folks, ahm getting ahead o masel here, hing oan tae ah get a swally.

'Aye pal a double an keep em comin, whits yer name son? James? Aw rats great. Get yersel wan, could be a long night. How much? Jesus Christ James, ah take it yer first name's Jesse. Aye, carry on son, ahm only jokin.'

Right, where wir we? Oh aye, so ahm at ma work an Benny says;

'Davie listen pal, since Senga done a runner wae yer cousin Luke, ye've no been oot the door. Noo, as a mate, dae ye no think it's time ye got yersel oot an aboot again, back in amongst aw they femme fatales.'

Honest injun folks, ah couldny hiv been listening, cos the next day Benny's sayin;

'That's you fixed up wee man, get yersel up tae The Ponderosa on Great Western Road this Friday night, an there's the perfect squaw comin your way.'

So before ah know it, ahm outside the door, and ah couldny find the gaff, so whenever ah asked folk they sniggered. Of course, when ah walked in ah could see why. It's only wan o them fuckin Wild West clubs, an here's me wae ma Hawaiian print shirt, an ma Adidas sambas oan. Whit is it they say. The only perfect vision is hindsight? Ah suppose the clues were all there, bit that Benny wan, he's jist too wide fir me. Mibbe they all are.

Ach well, here I am. Tell ye the truth. it's like a seventies social club, all dim lights, stale beer and glitterball. Wonder if cowboys play bingo? An then there's the music. These Cowboy clubs play the worst, feel-sorry-fir-yersel country songs ever. They've probably got their counsellors fir when they get suicidal. Ye can jist imagine it can't ye?

'Hi, we're the Samaritans Nashville, please step away from the juke-box and we'll talk some'

'Tell ye whit it is hen, it's ma wee cow pony, an he's actin so strange.'

Sir?

Aye, he knows that I'm restless oot here on the range.

Know something? This set-up reminds me o the old joke; Whit dae ye get if ye play a Country and Western song backwards? Well, ye get everything back. Ye get yer wife back, ye get yer weans back, ye get yer job back, ye get yer hoose back ye get yer dug back. Ah still think that's funny so ah dae.

So, ahm lookin at this poster on the wall advertising up-coming functions, and it says; Coming Soon, Johnny Cash Tribute Band. It made me giggle, ye see a few of my exes compared me to Johnny Cash. Aye, they were forever calling me Shorty Cash. Ended up calling me and ma mates Shorty Cash and the Giro-Bandits. In them days we jist laughed at everything.

'James, another large vodka pal, an get yersel another wan, seein as you've probably laughed at me the least.'

Anyway, the last thing that bastert Benny says is;

'Yer date says she'll be cairryin a paper under her arm an it will show ye that she has the same interests as you Davie boy.'

Noo, ahm a bit o a wan fir the gee gees, an ah thought, aye fair enough, so here I am, an in she comes an she's wearin aw this mad cowboy gear, well cowgirl gear. Noo, ah see the Racing Post under her arm, so ah know that it must be her. Then she turns roon, an we get a wee gander at her. Jesus Christ naw. There's folk turnin tae stone everywhere. Nae wonder she's got the Racing Post wae her, it's the fuckin family album.

'Heh Shergar, welcome back.'

Anyway, fir some reason she seems tae know who I am, cos up she comes an says;

'You must be Hawaiian Dave. Well, are ye?'

An ah says; 'Imma whit? Hawaiian Dave?'

So she comes back wae; 'Naw, ah KNOW yer Hawaiian Dave, are ye goin tae the bar?'

So right away ah knew this wid be a challenge. If there's wan thing worse than an ugly date, it's a cheeky ugly date. An ahve nae doubts she'll be sayin the same thing hirsel aboot me tae. Anyway ah say tae masel, Davie boy, yer gonny hiv tae fight fire wae fire here.

'Aye ahm goin tae the bar, an who are you? Catastrophe Jane?'

'Calamity pal, calamity.'

So ah turn roon an says aye your no kiddin hen, then ah shout; 'James, c'mon son, c'mon rob us again.'

See while aw this is goin on, ahm fuckin cursin that bastert Benny Boyle upside doon. Ah mean, it's bad enough settin me up wae A Fistful of Falsers here, bit tae no tell me it wis a Wild West night, well that wis lower than a sidewinders bawsacks. Aw Jeez, noo ahm beginning tae talk aw that cowboy stuff. It must be rubbin aff on me.

Mibbe it's a Glesga thing. Mibbe we hiv a spiritual connection wae the pioneerin frontiers people. Ah mean, ah no a few folk that think Dances with Wolves wis aw aboot Easterhoose. Glesga must be the only city in the world where the weans hiv moved on tae computers, bit the adults still play Cowboys an Indians. Anyway, Catastrophe has anither wee go at me when she says;

'So whits wae the Hawaii Five-O shirt? Ah take it the Five-O is yer age Granda?'

'Heard it Catastrophe, you knew Sitting Bull when he wis just a calf.'

'Ach ahm away tae the Ladies.'

'It's called the Squaws the night, an the gents is called the Braves.'

So, Catastrophe sashays away, an ye know something, she's actually a wee honey, especially when ye've switched over tae vodka vision. Bit ye know how these things work, ye never play yer cards too early in this game. Deep doon ahm wonderin if ah should jist cut ma losses when all of a sudden, a familiar face walks in the door. Aw Christ, it's Senga's wee sister Pandora, the only human being with the same DNA as a spittin cobra.

Don't get me wrong folks, it's nothin tae dae wae them cos we're divorced noo. But ah don't even want tae be here masel, and yit there's something weirdly fascinatin, watchin aw these adults actin oot their childhood fantasies. Anyway, ahm beginning tae think it's no ma night when James shouts on me an says;

'Here Davie, get this doon ye pal an get back in aboot it. She's playin hard tae get. Any western ahve ever seen, the guy disny get aff wae the burd till right at the end.'

James has restored ma faith in human nature, an the large vodka restores my courage tae, so ah say tae him.

'Hard tae get eh? Mibbe yer right James, bit ah think ahm gonny need a lasso fir this wan.'

Anyway, nixt thing, the band are givin it big licks tae 'Always on my Mind' and ahm feelin better, so ah turn roon tae see whits goin on the dance flerr, when a turn right intae this man mountain o a Sheriff an ah scale ma double vodka that James his bought me.

Aw Christ, ma fuckin vodka. Heh Sheriff whit you aw aboot?

Noo, it's no a big deal, bit ah wis raised tae no waste things, an although it's only a drink, it's still a waste. Anyway this brick shithouse turns an starts tae gie me this spiel, an ye want to hear this cowboy accent.

'Say dude, aint seen you around town much. And that aint the kind of language these ladies are used to hearing. Guess you're one of them sodbusters from back East?'

An ah thought, ah fuck it, if ye canny beat them, so ah came back wae;

'Aint that the truth now pardner, straight outa Calton.'

He disny know whether ahm joinin in wae him, or jist rippin the pish. So he his another go;

'People have got manners round here mister, don't need no city people coming in and upsettin us law-abiding folks with their fancy ways and speeches.'

Jesus Christ Almighty, this guys fir real, whit ahm ah gonny dae? An who comes waltzin back in but Catastrophe Jane, aw Jeez it's all getting on tap o me noo. Ahm too tired fir a barney so ahll try an talk ma way oot o this.

'Do your manners extend to an introduction Sheriff?'

'Why sure mister, the names Earp.'

He must hiv been practising that, cos his Texan drawl wis spot-on. The only problem here is that too often, ah lead wae ma lip. Especially when ma mooth's been dressed.

'You must be Quiet Earp? Ahve no heard aboot you.'

I knew it must have annoyed him cos he moved his waistcoat back so that ah could see his guns. Aw haud oan a minnit, there's something no right here, is this The Brokeback Mountain Cowboy Club? But this Sheriff wis no country bumpkin, he glances at my thinning hair and comes gallopin back wi this gem;

'Guess we could call you The Man With No Mane. Unless that is you want to tell these good folks who you are.'

Ach by this time ahm leathered wi the drink an am past carin, so ah stick ma chin oot and says;

'The name's Eastwood.'

Bit before ah can say anything else, the gila monster that is Pandora sticks her wee neb in an says;

'Aye that's right, Skint Eastwood.'

Catastrophe narrows her eyes towards Pandora an says tae her;

'Mibbe it's you that needs skint ya rattlesnake ye.'

Tell ye whit folks, Catastrophe has revived my droopin spirit wae her defence of me. Mibbe loud shirts, trainers and sweat dis something for her. Meanwhile, The Man Who Shot Liberty Bodice says;

'Maybe you should mosey on out of town stranger, these good folks don't need your sort around here.'

Fuck it noo, ahm wantin oot o here anyway, bit this bawbag isny gonny treat me like this jist because he's got wan o them stinkin badges.

'Ach ye said aw that earlier Sheriff, mibbe yer no from Deadwood efter all, mibbe yer really from Knightswood is that it? Mibbe this'll help ye. Dae ye mind that scene frae The Gunfight at the KO Corral?'

Ah can hear a few sniggers in the backgroon, bit that's fine, the merr the merrier.

'Say dude don't you mean The OK Corral?'

'Naw Sheriff, ah know exactly whit ah mean.' BANG. KEBLAMO.

Ah belted him right on the chin folks, an he must hiv caught his Cuban heels on the sticky carpet, cos he go's sprawlin over a table, drink ivrywhere.

'That's the best impersonation ahve seen aw night Sheriff. So it is'

Of course, every Sheriff has his deputies, and wan o them catches me a dull yin, so that's me on the deck as well. I look aboot me, Christ, the flerr's busy the night. Up in a flash and in time tae see Catastrophe catchin Pandora a belter and doon she goes. And here's whit a find amazing. As soon as ah hit the Sheriff, aboot three or four fights erupted at other tables. Mibbe it's a Glesga thing. Some people spontaneously combust, we spontaneously fight. Anyway, in the true spirit of the Titanic, the band play on. The lassie daein the singin is superb, she sounds like Shania Twain. Mind you she looks like Mark Twain.

So, she's beltin oot the old Billie Jo Spears song as everybody else is jist beltin oot. And in the middle of this riot I can feel somebody lookin at me. It's wee Catastrophe, and she's givin me a right beamin smile. So I nod towards the door and she nods back, and in seconds flat we're headin doon the steps oot intae Great Western Road. And the singer is givin it, 'What I've got in mind is to disappear, or maybe just stay right here, well to tell the truth what I've got in mind is makin' love to you.'

As we stroll towards the settin sun, I'm sayin tae masel, Jeezo, this is jist like wan o them Hollywood Westerns. But wee Catastrophe must be reading ma mind, cos she breaks the spell when she turns roon an says, 'Fancy a kebab?

Firhill

Stewart Sanderson

Under casual clouds, the roofscape brightening
on dark as the day moves down, the pitch proceeds
half heartedly at first. The score is what
it might be next, while the grace, the sweat, the bleed
do little more than run. These people move
and are not people – figments in the mind
impelling them on. But never enough to prove
controllable. The patterns half cohere
and never will: two colours half against
and half beneath the clouds. Owre rusted stands
this tension breaks.

Dog Days

HJ Rodgers

Dogs had to be kept inside that summer. The council ordered it. Eight foaming mouths and sixteen rolling eyes brought about a panic that saw armoured vans search the streets for strays. Sunlight strained through smeared windows, from where wet tongues and noses had pressed against the glass. Next door's elderly Border terrier, grey about the muzzle, watched his last June pass in silence. He never barked or whined; he just watched the world from his sofa-top seat. One Thursday morning, at 08:52, an infected dog threw itself onto the M8. With a single running jump it cleared the bridge's barriers and fell into the river of traffic below. The subsequent five-car pile-up made the national news, although the networks refrained from showing the aftermath of the disease-induced plunge. They said that feral canines were gathering on the banks of Loch Lomond, making ready to launch an attack on the streets of Glasgow, drawn by the scent of the half-eaten chips, kebabs and pakora that bred within the city's waste bins. But I was not afraid.

I watched a lot of TV that summer. I watched the World Cup because the tables and figures and matches gave a sense of order to my days. Three games a day meant four and a half hours without thinking. Five and a quarter if you counted half-time. Even longer if you watched the pre-match build up and the post-match analysis. My dreams were filled with the Dutch national team and rabid dogs.

Living in Glasgow felt like living in a bowl. The steep slope of the M77 and the steep slope of Earl's Seat made the borders. The hills marked the beginning of tourist-board Scotland, leading on to the Trossachs and those bonnie banks. But I couldn't climb those vertiginous sides; they seemed slick with a coating of old food and fat.

My CPN came on Mondays. 'Have you made plans to visit your family yet?' she said.

No, I said, not yet.

'Like we discussed last week? What about your sleep? How's that?'

The same as before, I said. She gave me some leaflets about a balanced diet and left.

If you go to the Kelvingrove they have a bit at the beginning about all the things that make up life in Glasgow. Sectarianism, domestic violence, poor mental health, country music. Honest, go on and have a look. Welcome to Glasgow. We hope you enjoy your stay.

I was washing up the pots from the tea and looking out of the window when I saw the dog, snuffling in the hedge at the bottom of the garden. I wasn't daft, I'd heard the news reports, but I wanted to see what it looked like before I rang the warden. I watched her chew a crust I'd thrown out for the birds the day before. She didn't look diseased. I've only got a small garden, a yard really, and I could see her eyes from where I stood and they looked bright and clear. A mongrel definitely but maybe her dad was a Yorkshire terrier because she wasn't much bigger than a cat. I opened the fridge and found some ham I'd been saving for dinner. I put a slice on a saucer, opened the back door and set it down for her. I waited.

She looked up when the key turned in the lock. Her gaze never left mine as she approached the meat. I stepped back to show her she could take it and she approached on tentative feet, until her twitching nose was near enough to give the plate a good sniff. Then she grabbed the ham with quick teeth and ran off, back under the bushes to where I knew there was a gap in the fence. Good luck lass, I thought.

I fell asleep on the sofa most nights. Usually woke at three to late-night shopping and subtitled films. I woke that night to a soft whining outside the back door. I walked through the darkened kitchen and opened the door to find her sitting on the step.

Come on then, I said, get on in before they catch you. She trotted in and sat on the lino while I filled a bowl with water. She lapped it up and I gave her a couple of digestive biscuits from the tin. What are we going to do with you then? I thought. She followed me into the living room, where the TV cast coloured light onto the walls. She jumped lightly onto the seat next to me, turned round three times and went to sleep.

A week passed. I got her a bone from the butcher's and she gnawed at it while I watched the football. I let her out on a piece of rope in the garden so she could do her business and at night she slept on the sofa with me. Her head rested on my foot and I could feel the steady small breaths on the skin between my sock and trouser leg. She liked catching grapes so I'd throw them up in the air and she'd gulp them down. Never knew a dog that liked fruit before. Monday came round again and so did the CPN.

'How're you getting on?' she said.

Fine, I said. I'd locked the dog in the upstairs bedroom. Didn't want anyone finding out about her.

'What about that trip to see your daughter?'

Not booked it yet, I said. But I will, I said. She nodded and looked in her bag for some more bloody leaflets to give me. A single bark sounded from upstairs.

'Was that a dog?' she said, looking surprised.

Next door's, I said. These walls are paper thin.

She started to put her jacket on. 'Shame,' she said, 'About the dogs. I used to have a border collie. The council's on about a city-wide cull next. Can't see that going down well.'

I showed her out and she said she'd see me next Monday. I went upstairs and the dog was sat on the bed, tail wagging. You nearly got us caught lass, I said.

She wasn't as used to staying indoors as me. Once the bone was gone she'd sit by the front door and whine, asking for a walk with those bright eyes. Her eyes spoke of running and chasing, of bounding over grass and splashing in streams. I felt bad cooping her up inside but there wasn't much I could do. The council had implemented the compulsory cull, despite opposition from animal rights groups. But public opinion swung in the council's favour when a dog bit a kid and caused the first case of canine-to-human rabies in a hundred years. After that the papers got behind the euthanasia.

It was one of the World Cup rest days when I decided to ring my daughter. She was living down in London, had done for the past three years. I'd never been south of Blackpool but my CPN seemed to think it'd be a good idea to visit her. And, I was thinking, it might be best to get the dog out of Glasgow.

'Hello?' she said, picking up the phone.

Hello love, I said, it's your Dad. I asked her what she was up to and how the job was going. I asked if she'd watched any of the football, she said no. I was thinking, I said, I might come and see you.

'It's a bit awkward at the minute,' she said, 'I have to go to Europe for a month.'

Oh, I said. Never mind, it was only a thought.

'Some other time,' she said, 'Just give me a bit more notice. Maybe in the new year?'

Aye, I said, that would be nice. She had to go and we said goodbye.

The dog was sat by the door, crying again. She deserves a good run outside, I thought. In the under stairs cupboard, under a pile of old coats, I found an old messenger bag. I tried her in it and she fitted easily. The outer flap meant she got plenty of air but stayed hidden from sight. I lifted her out again and she scampered round, wagging her tail. I went in the kitchen and got a plastic bag, filled it with her bowl, some meat scraps wrapped in tin foil, an apple for myself and a bottle of water for us to share.

On the bus to Buchanan Street I held the bag on my knee and she stayed quiet. I got off at the bus station and looked on the electronic boards for a bus that would take us north, perhaps as far as Rowardennan. We were in luck. There was one leaving in fifteen minutes that went via Alexandria. I popped my hand inside the bag and gave her ears a pet. A wet tongue licked my palm and I knew she was ok.

I watched the landscape change as we journeyed out of the city and into the hills. I'd forgotten how the country looked and I drank in the purple of the summer heather and the yellow of the gorse. I sat at the back undisturbed; the only other passengers were an elderly couple who occupied the front seats. They got off in Alexandria and we continued alone up the lochside road to Rowardennan. Good day to you, I said to the driver when we reached our stop. He nodded in return, closed the doors behind us and drove away.

We were at the base of Ben Lomond. Just a minute lass, I said, we'll make sure no-one else's about first. I'd found some old hiking boots in the cupboard and they were still a good fit. It was a clear day but because it was midweek there were no other walkers. Still, I walked for twenty minutes or so, up through the woods before I stopped to set the bag down. She scuttled out with a shake of her head and rolled on her back in the dead leaves. I laughed.

We never met anyone else the whole way up. She stretched her muscles, running off in front of me but always coming back if I disappeared from view. She sniffed along rabbit paths and marked her scent on tussocks of grass. The wind picked up and it made her even more playful, scampering up to me and barking before running off again. As her lungs expanded with the fresh air I felt mine do the same and I remembered walking this path as a young man. My stride grew more assured and I felt my back straighten in a way it hadn't for years.

I thought I'd find it a struggle but she kept me going. We reached the top and I allowed myself to turn round for the first time. I'd been saving the view for myself the whole way up.

My four walls had turned into a vast country. All around were hills and mountains, lochs and streams. No traffic, no houses, no people. Just me and the dog. She sat by my leg, leaning against me. I sat on a large flat rock and took the apple from my bag, giving her a scrap of meat and bowl of water. Just you and me lass, I said. Just you and me.

Last Orders

Laura Bissell

She walked into the pub and looked around. It was crowded. She glanced at the clock above the bar. Five to midnight. Should still get served. Susan moved towards the bar and nodded to the barmaid, a forty-something peroxide blonde with tired eyes and a fleshy face. Just a quick one eh? The woman laboriously moved herself from where she was leaning on the bar and walked towards Susan.

You'll need to be out by quarter past.

Aye that's fine.

You'll need to be drunk up by quarter past, y'understand or it'll get took aff ye.

Aye that's fine, I will be.

Dead eyes.

What you wantin?

A vodka thanks. Wi lemonade.

Her eyes panned around the bar. The lights were already up and folk were mainly standing with drinks in their hands talking loudly. It was crowded.

The woman set her drink in front of her.

Two pounds eighty.

The exchange of money, the momentary monetary transaction occurred.

She always felt a little apprehensive drinking alone in a pub. The feeling of being watched. Eyes on her, trying to suss her out. The feeling of unease. Of feeling noticeable. Conspicuous. Nobody staring at the many males sitting having a wee drink themselves. No bother for them. But for her, the eyes. The inquisitive looks. The more than inquisitive looks. The occasional approach. The odd lewd comment hollered across the pub. Always the feeling of unease. Unease in her own skin. Awkward. Everything was such an embarrassment, everything done with the feeling of not doing it quite right. She looked at the woman at the bar beginning to empty the drip trays. The flesh on her bare arms jiggled as she tipped them down the sink, and the brown dregs sloshed in the basin. A little of the liquid sloshed on her top but she didn't notice. I wonder if she feels like that thought Susan. I wonder if we are all the same, muddling through, trying to get by without embarrassing yerself any more that you have to. Oh lord, she was getting a bit deep fur this time of night. She took a sip of her drink. Cheap lemonade and cheap vodka, a sad shrivelled slice of lemon lobbed in for good measure.

She drank it quickly, almost in one go.

Same again.

The barmaid raised an eyebrow at the speed at which she had drunk her drink but began going through the motions of preparing her another.

Maybe she would have another after this, she thought. Just get absolutely fucked. Fucking boozed and obliterate all the thoughts that were going round in her head. What a fucking cliché, she thought, of the alcoholic intellectual, drowning one's sorrows. Not quite she thought. The alcoholic artist/intellectual is inevitably male. For her to drink means that she isnae coping, that she is unstable, that she is unwomanly. When McLean keeps a bottle of whisky in his desk drawer for 'occasions' (like a fucking Monday morning more like, thought Susan) if she were to do the same she would find the comforting arm of a member of the secretarial staff leading her out while the department stood around embarrassed for her, shaking their heads, tutting. Hypocrites she thought. The lot of them.

The barmaid plopped her abject looking drink on the bar, sloshing a substantial amount of it over the side in her gusto, and pretending not to notice.

Two pounds eighty, she said.

Cheers, said Susan. As the barmaid began to lumber away, Susan felt a desperate need for human contact, a sudden ache to have someone to talk to.

Busy tonight? She blurted.

No bad.

When did you start? Pathetic chat, she thought, fucking pathetic attempt at a conversation. She chastised herself.

Startit at six. The barmaid seemed quite content to have a break in the monotonous male company. But ah'm in first thing the morrow too. Always last wan oot and first wan in. She gave a weak smile.

Deliriously happy at having instigated a conversation, Susan struggled for the next step in this tête-à-tête.

Have ye worked here long?

It's amazing how one's middle class accent and one's first class honours degree English can so easily slip into the patois depending on the situation.

About a year, ventured the woman, and then conspiratorially, but ah'm looking for sumthing else n aw.

Oh right, said Susan. Why's that?

The woman began blethering about the hours and her children and how she would rather not work such late nights and how her partner couldn't get work at the moment because of his line of work and the recession and how he didn't like her working night anyway but he'd never get a job in a bar or anything like that so surely he cannie say that she shouldnae do it when they need the money and…

As the woman's words washed over her, Susan thought about how she hadn't really wanted to talk at all and how looking at this woman, who was older than her, standing at midnight in a bar serving a bunch of lewd men and her while her kids were at home, was fucking unbearably sad. Sometimes the pathos of life astounded Susan and she felt her body go limp at the sudden feelings of sadness and abjection.

She made some consoling noises and took the last gulp of her drink.

That's a real shame, she managed to mutter before putting her glass on the bar and turning on her heels. The barmaid who was mid-flow stopped mid sentence, mouth slightly open and watched her leave, before sighing and picking up the empty glass on the bar.

Once she was outside Susan took a big gulp of air. The two drinks she had downed in quick succession had gone to her head. She leaned her hand against the cool tiles at the side of the pub entrance. Glancing towards the distant lights of the Barrowlands she pulled her collar up around her face and headed in the opposite direction down the Gallowgate, her arm hovering, ready to signal for a taxi.

The Urban Myth

Rachel Tennant

Glasgow the glorious – the glaikit:
the big hearted, cholesterol hardened,
fat capital of the commonwealth.
Glasgow the generous – the mean fisted:
the epi-centred, epi-guttural,
gutter trash city of culture.
Glasgow the red – but dead Clyde:
cheek-by-jowl, tongue-in-cheek,
Celtic Park versus Bard-in-the-Park.
Glasgow the victorious – the vanity insanity:
the Doges Palace, Egyptian Halls,
Trinity Towers and brash city malls.
Glasgow the glamorous – the glitzy:
the emerald veined, methadone drained,
Style-Mile metropolis of Scotland.
Glasgow the greened – the begrimed:
the dear space, heard-hearted place,
my bewitched-bewildered urban myth.

Glasgow

Alan Riach

Glasgow is the best of plays: you can act in it and watch it at the same time.
Edwin Morgan

1

The narrow path leads down on the diagonal, close to the wall.
Intimate enough to see the fossil strata, the wisps of grass, what life
Insinuates its roots into the fissures, holds on, grows its green out upwards from the shadow,
And how the shadows fall across the canyon walls, and slowly lean and move across
Their textures, as the sun does its old arc thing once again. You move in closer when
The mule brigade ride up and want to pass, flatten yourself against the vertical
Plane behind you, watch them place their sure hoofs near the edge.

2

Thus I was in Arizona, years ago. Today, the pleasure on the path and edges of
The city is the same: a history of stories getting deeper in a walking world
Or maze of traffic made for circling, zig-zags, ziggaruts, explorable depths
And heights that show you out across the world in blue. Let's list a few.
One Sunday afternoon down by the Clyde, walking past the statue with her arms
Raised to remember the reason why the Spanish Civil War was fought, we came
To the Finnieston Crane, no-one around and the small gate in the fence unlocked.

3

We went up. Steel steps took us to the top, but standing on the horizontal there,
I saw a further ladder on the side wall of the cabin, got to the roof. And smoked a cigarette,
Looking around. The rooftops all before you and blue all the way to Arran, Ayrshire, South.
The conurbation, East. The Islands, West and North, and mountains in the North-West, through
The gap at the end of the Great Western Road, that leads you to the Gaeltacht,
By the pass of the Camel's Hump. Came down again and walked back into town.
Co-ordinate points, a history, a sense of what you still believe is: inextin guishable, live.

4

Scenic? Hardly. But nevertheless. What archeology supplies sets layers and connections in
The mind. What's now? Bridges and the river still, the skyline: Scott's Gothic tower points up like
Aspiration, spaceship-sharp; so much else points down, is earthed and mobile, Dennistoun bars and
West End brasseries. Take off the top of your skull and open your brain to the air: let's go
For the open-topped tour. Victorian Glasgow: George Square and grandilo quence, architecture
Rising and ornate, that flourishes its culmination in the Art School on its own diagonal, steep.
Below that, Merchant City, slave trade and tobacco lords, and money building East End

5

Market manners, commerce, a deep exchange of language, a currency we trade in, even now.
Below that, the Cathedral and the crypt to mark old Mungo and his long ago approach
To the Molendinar Burn, the water now to be seen only in a well up in Blackhill. But it's
The mix of the thing, the shoulders rub together, the acting as you walk and watch, the lifting
Of concern, the taking part: looming on that green-roofed, narrow-spired Cathedral is
Victoria's Infirmary, a massive block of stone and glass opaque with grime, and looming over both,
From further East, the shadowy Necropolis, the village of the dead, with John Knox high

6

On pillar at its summit, arm stretched out, in supplication? benison? Deer and foxes roam here now.
That's good. But not enough. Under that there's more. Just fourteen feet below St Vincent Street:
The carboniferous. Such knowledge as the strata bring began for me in childhood, walking with my
Papa from railway to bookshop to shop, arcade to arcade, where colours were bright on covers and
Spines and diamonds, and language spoke with beguilment, on pages and in air. Conversations
Made and make the space work bright: what seams streak through pollutions of the bad beliefs,
Bodies made to end in haste and unfulfilment, the pathos now itself cliché, industrial and after that.

7

So, not nostalgia, please. What is so sad and cannot now be claimed, is unreturnable.

Recognise that. Dividedness, and not diversity. It's there all right. But when
you feel this city work,
As a friendly force that drives the green life up and out of the earth, the air
enamelled blue
With all the conviction of speech in its best gambols, it's something worth a
listen to and look
Around, and colourful, as Doré's Dante's deep Inferno, keeps you guessing,
horrified, for people,
And knowing that the love and laughter, light, are in there too, right to the
end.
From far beginnings we might never know, but what the present is, is what
we do.

Morgan Orbital

Alan Riach

Over Rutherglen: Cathkin Braes. Begin with the curvature of earth, rising on your way south-east, landing at a spot exactly on the round, bald brow of the place, and turn to look over the whole various city in its cradle of the Valley Clyde, the hills all louping round it in their whiteness like a school of whales, breaching, sounding, rising, diving, and Ahab-like, a charting, hunting, endless, set determination, not to fix on one but find as many as the shapes and slopes are different in movement, action, form. He walked the incline over Cathkin Braes, talking with his friend of what was yet to come.

Come into the arcana of the Gothic castle: literature and languages, built on infinite strata of scrap, colours everywhere, structures of all kinds. With others, building bridges into strangeness, what dimensions world war brings to those whose hearts are bound to letters not to violence. And the grey fog falls in city canyons, the riverwater slugging through the channels and the ships blast out their horns at midnight once a year in multitudes of tones. His ears tune in to levels. Register, translate, make sense of wordless songs and dumb desires. Russian sounds and looks as far removed, as close connections are in energy alive.

Alive as a string from a rod in the still, slow stream: the worm on the hook, the hook on the line, the line along the long bamboo, the fingertip alive to it. And then, the tug. The whole earth, curve and mass, solidity, begins its move in the astronomical dark. The stars light up co-ordinates. You have it at your muscle's call, the poise and strength is there to make your strike. North-east to Glasgow Green, the company of men unseen, unseeded in the dark. The east end beckons, the workers sleep below the pavement marked to tell us all at Candleriggs. Above Cathedral and Necropolis, the ponderous approach: Tarkovsky in his great balloon is coming down to visit.

Visit north and then to Anniesland, along Great Western Road, curved like a drumlin runway for the off. Take the top flight on the bus, sit at the front and see the future coming from the height. South-west, along the estuary, old Dumbarton rock, Clydebank, Davidson and Graham then and all those city boys were pointing towards, the rivets, facts and language going in like nails into the hardwood planks, then east again, and back towards where it was you started from, where was it now? The loss of yourself in city, cities, let it be as always in the labyrinth, the thread that takes you into more than one road, corridor, avenue, around, to find yourself in difference, and over.

Leabhar air a' Ghàidhealtachd san Uinneig

Aonghas Mac Leòid

Tha seann Ghàidheal na ghurraban
san uinneig air Sràid Bhochanain
's e feuchainn ri creic leabhraichean
airson bodach à Wolverhampton.

Chaidh e mu thuath an toiseach
airson tràth fhada air falbh
bhon latha seo th' ann,
is e air sgrìob gu Tìr nan Òg
air a chapall bhàn:
stad e a charavan
os cionn tràigh ìomhagach
far 'n do rinn e gàire, thog e dealbh
is chuir e a champ an òrdugh.

Aig ceann thall a bhliadhna chruaidh
(is e fearail mar na tùsanaich)
thog e thoman uaine,
far an cromadh e ri chluasag,
far nach truailleadh garbh-ghaoth
an t-saoghail an starsnaich.

–Nis, cà bheil na fir-chlis ghasta
a ghin na bodaich san taigh-òsta?
cuiridh mi duanag an òrdugh
a sheinneas an cuid cliù,
is a thromaicheas mo phòca'.

Birlinn is birlinn eile air triall do
thìr an àigh, le pailteas soirbheis
air an cùlaibh: calpa na luing ud
a' sìor mheudachadh, sa chiaradh.

Highland Books in the Window

Aonghas Mac Leòid

The old fella sitting squat
in the Buchanan Street
window, trying to sell books
for a Wolverhampton gadgie.

He went up North at first
for a long spell away
from today, heart made up
on a Land of Youth
astride a white horse:
he stopped his Pegasus caravan
above chesspiece sand
where he smiled and caught a picture
and set his camp in order.

At the far end of a long year
(now as manly as the natives)
he built up his wee green hill,
where he'd curl up to a pillow
where the roughwind of the world
does not swing the threshold.

- Now, where are those Northern dancers
conceived by those oldtimers in the inn?
I'll put together my own folksong
that sings of feats, of deeds
and weighs my pocket down.

Birlinns, and other charters on the books,
skimming over to the land of joy, profitable
gusts behind them: riggin' growing
darker in the twilight.

SNAZZY HEADGEAR DUDE.
GLASGOW CITY CENTRE.
TUESDAY NIGHT, 9PM.
GLASWEGIAN COUTURE.
I THINK HE'D LOOK BETTER IN YOUR HAT!
NO WAY.
EXCUSE ME...
'HUV YE GOT ANY MONEY' YE COULD GIE US A LOANA?
I'M SORRY PAL - BUT WE DONT HAVE ANY CASH.
YA SEE.. WE'RE GOIN FER AN INDIAN TAKEAWAY AND WE WANT TAE GET A PESHWARI NAN BREAD WI IT, BUT THATS FANCIER THAN A NORMAL NAN - SO ITS MORE EXPENSIVE SEE... A PESHWARI NAN HAS GOT ALMONDS AND STUFF INSIDE IT, BUT WE'RE A POUND SHORT 'COS WE'VE ONLY GOT ENOUGH FER A NORMAL NAN.

WE'RE PURE STARVIN FER A PESHWARI NAN 'COS THEY'RE THAT TASTY MAN, YA KNOW?
GUYS, WE REALLY DONT HAVE ANY CASH... SORRY.
EH....
'ARIGHT - CHEERS THEN. MIND' TRY WAN A' THEY NANS WHEN YE CAN A'RIGHT?
I'M DYING FOR A PESHWARI NAN NOW.
ME TOO.

The Wrong Man

Brian Hamill

He wanders into Central Station and looks up at the boards. His train isn't leaving for a while yet; there's time to nip to the toilet. He goes down the stairs, trusting his feet to feel for the steps while he looks in his bag for the money. Thirty pence. He shakes his head.

There is some noise coming from the gents, raised voices as he approaches. He walks quickly through the sink area and makes for a cubicle. A fat man wearing a linen suit and a straw hat is rubbing round his face with paper towel as he passes, scraping his little goatee beard dry.

Look at this fat fucking explorer here.

Ha ha!

As he slips into the cubicle he notices two teenagers in tracksuits sitting on the counters next to the sink. One is fully up there, his back resting against the wall and his trainers placed right in the bowl. The other one has a baseball cap on and his legs are dangling off the countertop.

Haw Jumanji, where you aff tae dressed lik that? You goin oan safari?

Naw naw, he's away tae git that fannyhair shaved aff iz chin.

Their laughter echoes round the tiled room, then dies down. Presumably, the fat man has made a sharp exit. He does up his fly, sighs, checks his watch. The train is leaving in three minutes. He wrestles his way out of the narrow cubicle with briefcase in hand, and walks smartly towards the exit.

For a second, he thinks he's been too quick for them again and is going to sneak past unnoticed. Just as he nears the exit, the baseball cap jumps off the counter and into the doorway.

Excuse me.

Whit.

Sorry but I've got a train to catch, excuse me please.

He tries to squeeze by the boy, who sidesteps in front of him again, leaving no space.

Haw Cheezy, look at this clatty cunt tryin tae leave withoot washin iz hawns.

The other one swivels and lifts his feet out of the sink so he's facing them.

Wash yer fuckin hawns.

Look I have to go now or I'll miss my train, let me by.

No fuckin way pal. You could be goin aboot geein people diseases n that. Right Snedders?

Too fuckin right mate.

Let me by, for fuck sake!

Ooh! Comin the hard man now ir ye? Whit you gonnae dae, wipe yer shitey hawns oan me? Cheezy, start the wahter.

This really isn't funny, I've got to get on that train.

Look boss, yer washin they fuckin hawns before ye go anywhere, an that's fuckin that.

The man looks at the boy. The boy looks back at the man, grinning.

Oh for God's sake, you bloody fucking idiots!

He frantically rolls his sleeves up and rushes over to the sink with the running water. It is scalding hot, so he mixes it with the cold, rubs some liquid soap on, rinses, dries them quickly on his trousers, and sprints for the door.

All the while, the two are laughing and making jokes, and when he leaves they shout after him:

Ma wean's fuckin four yir auld and she knows tae wash ur hawns.

Ye can afford a fancy suit but ye go fur a pish and then stoat back oot intae the street, ya manky bastard.

Filthy boggin mingin dick-hawns!

The man clambers up the stairs, sweat already showing on his face. He hears a whistle, but is still scanning the boards when his train begins to pull away from the platform.

He looks up to the high roof of the station, letting out a moan of disappointment. Then stands, looking for the time of the next departure and trying to catch his breath. He turns and walks over to the coffee shop, and buys a large black coffee and a slice of carrot cake. The carrot cake is eaten immediately, the wrapper left lying on the counter.

He takes the coffee back onto the station floor. As he does so the two boys emerge from the toilet, and make for a side exit. He can see they're still laughing and talking as they do so. He follows them onto the exit stairs, speeding up so he can catch them before they reach the street.

The baseball cap notices the footsteps and turns around.

Excuse me. You know you made me miss my train with all that bloody nonsense?

They are both facing him, smiling.

Are you fuckin serious pal?

Yes I'm serious. It was very important I get on that train. You shouldn't have done that.

The two stare at each other, open-mouthed, ready to laugh.

Mate, ye do realize that yir gonnae get yer fuckin cunt kicked right in, don't ye?

You don't give a toss about anyone else. Scum, that's what you are. Both of you. Fucking scum of the earth.

The boys are frozen for a second, then the baseball cap lunges up at the man. Before the other boy can reach them, the baseball cap falls backwards screaming in pain. While the other boy looks to see what's happened, he gets the other half of the coffee square in the face.

Both of them reel to the floor in agony, screaming. The baseball cap's voice has broken into no more than a shriek. He cowers against the wall covering his face with both hands.

The man looks down at them, brandishing the steaming cup like a weapon.

You made a mistake, didn't you? You made a bad mistake.

He senses noise from within the station. The man drops the cup and jogs down the stairs and out into the street. The boys are still prostrate and whining, hiding their faces, when two men in Scotrail uniforms run into the stairwell.

By the time they can coax the boys into whispering what had happened through their scorched, aching lips, the man is in a taxi moving away from there, fast.

Glasgow Uni

Theresa Muñoz

there goes
my coat sleeves

soaked by cars
along Kelvin Way: a street

of dark puddles,
the gutters stuffed with leaves

*

sitting in class
I notice

each body in this lecture hall
is like mine:

legs crossed,
leaning forward

chin in palm,
glossy-eyed

*

first on tiptoe
then crouched down

I push left, then right
flick through the spines

searching for a book
I can't find

on the library's ninth floor,
late at night

*

beer mats, crisp bags
and foamy pints

appear on the table
then get replaced

in the blurred thrill
of our drinking

I lose all sense of time

*

I grip my pencil
with sweaty fingers

when my exam gets slapped down
I whisper, thank you

I look out the window
for answers

as the sun sinks lower

over the university tower

*

under the leafy arch of trees
the sound of the river
follows me

past the empty playgrounds
the cement skate park

still trying to get used
to the new routine

each day different
each day new

Close

Theresa Muñoz

huddled, cold
in a cave

of smooth tenement
brick

watching

brief wet textures fall
diagonally

like lines

drawn solid
across paper

a way

of cross-hatching
the air

Blue Shirt

Jamie Pilc

It occurred to me one day that things go in cycles. While the phrase might have some universality as a maxim, the example which had made me think of the thing was in fact made as an observation on my own patterns of thought. For example I will admit that, directly after I thought this, I questioned whether it were in fact true, as the sentence as an entity all to itself did not follow its own law. This brought me back to the sentence and instigated a frantic search for a way in which to edit it so that it had the effect of reading as something in the process of being constantly turned over. My failure in the proceeding seconds in this respect led me to consider that the phrase was not barren in truth, but perhaps to general and thankfully, that I might leave it at that.

Lying in an overflowing bath, the heat of which was making my head spin, a second thought occurred to me. I confidently suggested to myself that I would like it if I had a blue shirt to wear. Regardless of colour, a shirt is no use to somebody immersed in water, so I clearly did not intend that it should appear on my back at that very moment. The thought lingered however, passing inevitably through a screening of its level of cyclicity before I could ponder on it further.

When the screening proved inconclusive I was free to pursue the matter. I did not own a blue shirt at the time. My wardrobe housed a number of sleek white shirts from previous employment as a waiter, which I now had rare occasion to wear, and at least three of the checked, thick variety. It was here that I found myself mistaken, for indeed one of those checked, lumberjack shirts was blue in colour. I was then momentarily saddened to find that I congratulated myself on making such progress in my own mind as to recognise that this most probably meant that, beyond desiring a blue shirt, it was a certain sort that I was after. I will now relate that the efforts I made to acquire a blue shirt that fitted my requirements, and how these got somewhat out of hand.

The first mistake I made was to go to a shop the very next day and buy a blue shirt, though it is not difficult to see the logic in my action. It was not that the shirt I bought myself was not of good quality, as it happens I spared little expense. The thanks I got for such financial enthusiasm was that, on the breast pocket of my purchase, there was sewn the shape of a bear, around the size of a capital D. I assumed that it must have been a polar bear, for it was white as befitted the blue sky of the shirt and, though I do not think I was aware of it at the time, had passed through my mind as slight compromise against what otherwise appeared exemplary. The trouble with it, aside from that I wore it on a rather mild day, was that it seemed the bear annoyed me. It is not that I have any enmity towards bears; I think them magnificent creatures and am always struck, should I spot one, in how much they resemble dogs at certain points. In hindsight, I remember that, during that one day I wore the shirt, I came to fervently wish to be quit of the bear, even if this meant that he was only to turn into the outline of a dog in the same place. I wanted rid of him. There is a chance, I suspect, that had it not been for the bear and the angst he caused me, I should have gone through the rest of the time spent upon my quest in some labour entirely different from the one in which I did. There was, as I have said, another factor which coloured my view of the shirt with the bear on it: that I wore it on a mild day. Distracted as I was by the wildlife, I made less of the fact that, as the day grew mild enough for someone hasty to call it warm, the shirt stuck to me uncomfortably. Throughout that day as I went about my business, lingering in quiet spots for periods in which to ponder (and often glancing with concern at my breast pocket), I found I felt vaguely disgruntled. I do not fault the day itself, though there have been better ones in terms of what filled it and of my mood and though it cannot have been wholly the cause, there have certainly been better days on which I could have worn that shirt. Having just finished an espresso in a café professing to be Italian and noting the time, I resolved to return the shirt from whence I had come to have it in the first place. The young lady in the shop, the same who had sold the shirt to me that morning, was dressed from knee to neck in a close fitting piece of material which bore the pattern of an unusually uniformly striped zebra. I had observed that morning, and did so again now, that the pony tail of hair, perched almost atop her head, swayed and jerked around in time with whatever she was saying. Distorting her dense facial make-up, she frowned and reluctantly refunded me. I returned to my apartment, with its views of the town, and as I undressed some hours later to re-enter the bath, the same two thoughts from my last immersion reappeared.

Having enjoyed a lean breakfast in the excitement of the morning chill as it was felt upon my balcony, I found that I had decided what to do. It was by that point evident that I am the sort of man who has an innate selectiveness when seeking an item of attire. With equal clarity I considered not only that the shirt I sought did not have any sort of insignia upon it, but that I would likely also find fault with numerous other issues. For instance I feared that I might be plagued by a checked detail within the collar, a poorer cut than that of my first attempt, or with an uncomfortable label at hip level or perhaps reliance on cuff links, of which I own not one.

It was not until I leant a second time that morning into the fresh air which oxygenated the town that I decided my second course of action. There was a tailor located on a nearby street which also housed a bakery, one in which I sometime have occasion to, I suppose, vent my disdain for low-fat foods by availing myself of at least two Danish pastries. On entering the former establishment, I found it rather dark and was greeted unenthusiastically by a gentleman of advanced years whose ethnic origin I had no success in placing throughout our interview. My postman delivered the result a week later, retaining as he did so his title of the eldest human I have ever met prone to going about in shorts during such cold mornings as those.

I was horribly disappointed with the shirt. The tailoring shop's poorly lit interior had led me to select a shade of blue with a somewhat varnished look to it, or at least some trait which leant it a synthetic appearance to my eyes. Additionally, the buttons were ill placed, the second-to-top one being almost upon my windpipe, and the third-to-top button unopenable without requiring a medallion to nestle in the chest hair rendered visible and, if this were to be, a marked change in my personality. I spent the rest of the day garbed in my aforementioned blue checked shirt. Unfortunately, as I was considering that it was doubtful the tailor had any so lenient returns policy as I had previously been exposed to (especially as I am suspect the word he muttered as I passed through the door of the shop had been a disparaging one) taking my frustration into account when dressing that day in the end proved of little help to my state of mind. I passed the day until its evening in solitude, my pacings, abstractions and musings keeping the pulse only of the chill on the balcony when I ventured to it every hour or so. It was growing dark and I was approaching the lamented end of a hearty evening meal, when two gentlemen of my acquaintance made impressions upon the button at the door of the building I reside in.

An Sàr Shaighdear Havel

Calum MacLeòid

(mar chuimhneachan air Roinn Eòlas Slàbhaich, O.G.)

Bha sinn a' tilleadh bho mhargaidean Nollaige
gàirdeanan làn dhèideagan
cinn làn medovino
nuair a thòisich cluig nan cathrach a' brùthadh
agus sluagh a' tighinn còmhla air Ceàrnag Wenseslas
le aodainn sòlaimte
le brataichean mheileabhaid
le coinnlean shaora
le dìtheanan plastaige
agus le sàmhchair.

Bodhar le Anglicky,
cha do thog mi na co-dhùnaidhean ceart bho na tachartasan.

Shaoil mi gu b 'e dìreach,
uill, seòrsa de thraidisean a bh' ann
dòigh aca an Ceathramh Dòmhnach
den Aidbhein, 's dòcha, a chomharrachadh.

Thill sinn chun taigh-òsta
chùm iad orra a' leantainn
na rathad
gu coisrigeadh leaghadh oifis an leaghaidh.

The Good Soldier Havel

Calum MacLeòid

(In memory of the Slavonic Studies Department, G.U.)

We were returning from Christmas Markets
arms full of toys
heads full of mead
when the cathedrals bell's began tolling
and a crowd gathered on Wenceslas Square
with solemn faces
with velvet flags
with cheap candles
with plastic flowers
and with silence.

I assumed it was
well, sort of a tradition
their way of marking the last
Sunday of Advent.

Deaf by English
we didn't draw the correct conclusions from events.

We returned to our hotel
and the crowd continued
on his road
the inauguration of the liquidation of the liquidation office.

The Second Coming

Sophie Sexon

I have grown proud with Glasgow.
As a mother grows with child
I birth my own birthplace
Uncovering my late birthrights.

I had to see this city as a tourist:
I first abandoned her concretely, resolutely,
A city marked by that which never
I grew out of it.

The wee birds at the dancin'
The Belle on Great Western Road
Ah'm out ma tree
Gaunny gee us a fish supper

Characteristically, categorically, allegorically, literally
I had missed the point.
I moved to London.
I became homeless.

And I had to become homeless twice
Literally, allegorically, characteristically, categorically,
to realise I wasn't home.
Hame is where the heart is.

Glasgow begins again,
birthing anew a new birthright for me
My sons and daughters running

Like words like echoes through the streets
A way a lone a last a loved a long the
Forth and Firth
Now my first
Choice, my only Choice, my riverrun.

A Thousand Deaths

David Gourlay

Ricky Temple ran up the stairs, warming up so he'd be ready. He'd been here a few times and knew that the top two flats were boarded up, their front doors sealed with steel plate to keep out the scum. When he got to the second floor, flat on the left, he gave the door three loud bangs then stuffed his baseball cap in his pocket. After a few moments he stepped back and shoulder charged the door. The lock popped with a metallic ping. There was a shriek from inside.

Ricky ran in the direction of the noise and found her cowering beside the couch in the living room. The TV was on so he turned the volume up and stood over her.

She wouldn't look at him so he encouraged her by grabbing her face, his thumb and fingers digging into her cheeks.

'Hello Shona.'

She stared wide eyed at him, her mouth forced open by his grip. Her colour was bad and she smelled unclean. Disgusted, he pushed her back, banging her head against the wall. She grunted and curled up again. Ricky stood and looked around the room. It was a mess, and he wondered if he was wasting his time.

'How much you got?' No answer. Her bag was lying on the couch, so he tossed it, but her purse was empty. 'You're taking the pish! Speaking of pish, you fucking stink of it. Why don't you have a wash or somethin'. Go out and do a couple of old farts and pay me in the morning. It's a hundred, and rising.'

Her head bobbed up and down rhythmically. He didn't know if she was agreeing or silently sobbing, so he kicked her. She curled even tighter, trying to disappear. Her gear was lying all over the coffee table.

'In the meantime.' He started to gather it all up. One unopened packet went in his pocket and he carefully swept all the loose powder into his hand along with the syringes and other kit. She reached out a hand. 'Fuck off,' he said then went to the bathroom and flushed it all away, using a toilet brush to make sure. She hadn't moved, so he grabbed her hair and pulled her head back. 'Tomorrow it's the money, or we're getting into it.'

Before going out into the street he took a quick snort of coke. He had another small time pusher to threaten for one of the big boys, so he headed into town.

Neil Paterson got off the train in Central Station and headed for the downstairs exit. As he left the shelter of the Heilanman's Umbrella, he turned up the collar of his coat. He was supposed to be Christmas shopping but the recent death of his mother had left him a bit stunned and unmotivated.

'Excuse me... sorry.' The streets were busy. Neil did more than his fair share of stepping aside. He sighed at himself. Glasgow, city of the hard man; but he had been forged by a hard woman.

His mother was boss and brooked no challenge. His father, long gone. She prided herself that she had done a good job as a single parent. Her children behaved. When he had started to grow into a man, she had tried to take the place of his missing father and teach him how to deal with the world head on, but she had already stamped out the spirit he would have needed for it. Confrontation, or even the thought of it, left him weak. Neil kept himself fit, but his muscles turned to water in the face of a challenge. He blamed her, for keeping him clamped down for too long, so that he would never rise to her. But now she was gone. She was always too proud to admit to herself that her condition made her weak. The rich food she enjoyed only beckoned forth the heart disease that often followed in the footsteps of diabetes. He had only finished clearing out her house that week.

Neil was tired of dodging other shoppers so stepped up to the window of a jeweller's at the end of the Argyle Arcade. He stared in, pretending to window shop.

Ricky walked into the Solid Rock and saw a deal going down straight away. He thought an undercover cop would have a field day. The guy in the leather jacket, Nichol, the one he had been sent for, made eye contact with another guy in an orange hoodie. Hoodie raised his head in the inverted nod that meant business everywhere in the world. Nichol did the same and they headed for the toilets. Ricky casually picked up an empty glass as he followed.

Nichol went in first but Ricky stopped the other one. He frowned up at Ricky, but Ricky leaned in and gave him the look. Hoodie dropped his gaze and backed off. Nichol frowned slightly when he saw only this stranger behind him. Then he noticed how he was looking at him, and started sidling toward the door.

Ricky grabbed him by the throat and slammed him up against the wall. Nichol looked like he was about to throw a panicked punch, so Ricky closed his grip on his neck and changed his mind. Ricky showed him the glass then pressed it into his cheek with dangerous force.

'Do you have any idea who's asked me to pay you this wee visit?' There was a restrained nod. 'You never work the town again. He told me to make sure you took this tellin', cause next time I've to tie you up and chuck you in the Clyde.' Ricky lowered the glass and released him. 'So we're clear?'

Nichol was nodding and rubbing his neck.

'Ah know ah wiz chancin' it a bit…'

Ricky punched him fast between the ribs. Nichol gasped and folded to the floor.

'Good boy.'

Ricky put the glass in the sink and searched the near unconscious Nichol. He took his money and stash, then treated himself to another little snort before leaving. He noticed it was getting dark outside. Dark was his favourite time of day.

Neil was staring a million miles through the diamonds in the window when the street lights came on and stirred him. He looked up the street and immediately saw the big guy with the baseball cap. He looked set to take on the world. Neil looked away, then had the uncomfortable feeling that he recognised him from somewhere. He took a sidelong glance to check and saw him barge straight through an elderly couple who were coming the other way. The old lady was knocked to the ground.

'Bastard!' her husband shouted and tried a punch but was grabbed instead. 'Just see to yer wife ya auld fuck.' But he still looked set to deliver a punch. The younger man's eyes glazed.

Neil moved before he thought. His arms felt weak, but when the assailant made to punch the old man Neil felt like he stepped through a membrane. His arms and legs felt real and in the world again.

The thug didn't see Neil's punch coming. It caught him square, just above the cheek bone, and he staggered. Neil put another in the same place, and he started to go down. He let go of the man and grabbed at Neil's coat. They fell together, wrestling. Neil saw him grab for something in his pocket, so wrenched his hand free. Little packets of white powder sprayed out and a knife clattered away. Neil saw a young boy bend to pick it up, but his mother stopped him. So he put his foot on it instead. Neil lost his grip.

'Hoy you two!'

Neil felt his enemy's arms around him, fumbling. Suddenly the police were there, separating them. Neil's heart was hammering as he was pulled off by one of the officers. He felt greatly relieved at their presence.

His adversary started to struggle. The officer holding Neil told him not to move and went to help her colleague. They got him cuffed but he still had a lot to say for himself.

'He's a drug dealer,' he glared at Neil, 'he offered me drugs and threatened me with a knife. Search him, you'll see.'

Neil saw the old man step away from his wife.

'This lad helped me,' he said, pointing to Neil. Then he looked at the man in handcuffs. 'He knocked my wife down and was going to thump me. This is his stuff.' He pointed at the packets on the ground.

The boy spoke up.

'And this is his knife.' He kicked it forward and then pointed at Neil. 'He's the good guy.'

Neil had abandoned all thoughts of Christmas shopping and decided to deliver the last box of his mum's stuff. Everything else was in the charity shop or the skip.

When he saw the door ajar and the splintered frame his mind raced. 'Shona!' He found his sister sitting cross legged on the couch, crying into her hands. There was a fresh bruise on her leg. He dropped the box on the table and tried to comfort her, but she pushed him away.

Over a cup of tea she told him she was in trouble and it would be worse tomorrow. Neil started to panic and paced the room, his hands thrust into his coat pockets. He felt the little packets and stopped, trying to work out what they were. Then he remembered the thug's arms around him, fumbling, and then telling the police to search him.

'You've always got money. Give me the money I owe, and enough for some stuff. C'mon please this time, I need it.'

Neil knew that drugs were her way of rebelling against Mum, which was more than he had ever done, but he'd never given her money. He looked at the box he'd brought. Nothing that she could sell. Just some old photos, Mum's warm gloves and scarf, her tortoise shell hairbrush, and at the bottom a zippered little case that he'd thought was her travel toiletries. But now he remembered.

She had told him never to touch it because of the sharp needles, but little boys are curious and he had liked the way the plunger slid in and out of the heavy glass syringe. It was her very first insulin kit. She never threw anything away.

He felt the packets between his fingers and wondered if any of them were heroin.

'Look Shona, I can help you.' He crouched down in front of her. 'It can be what you want right now, or something better. It'll be your choice. She's gone now.' She looked at him.

'Something happened today. I did something I never thought I'd be able to. Let me tell you, and then you can choose.'

Sauchiehall Street

Ellen McAteer

After a long time
of bare concrete and branches
the sun's touch quickens
my cold eye

to the proud blue bloom
of an artificial flower
on a chemo-barren skull

to the tree of a man
bowed
under one budding son and
bound groundwards
by the bramble arms
of another

to the beautiful saxophonist
murdering jazz
and the freak shufflestepping
beside him

it would take Howson
to arrest their solid forms

I can only hope
to root this wee miracle
in the mind of another:
Spring has come to my gaze again.

Found in Translation

Ellen McAteer

"O! Look at the spider, knitting his net," you cried,
getting the alliteration, but shaking the cobwebs
out of a language you feared you would never learn.

Oh, never learn! It was as if your eyes were rinsed to childish clarity
by tears you had wept while reading me poems of Palestine;
as if your mouth made pictures, bright in primary colours,
of things I had only seen in shades of Glasgow grey.

I can hear music in your voice though I struggle to understand the words
as you read me "*Bitaqat huwiyya*", and the music of your language
leaks into mine, an Afro-Celt dance mix heard on the radio:
weaving webs of words linked not by sense but sound; a mother-tongue
that sounds like a mother, heard by a baby who cannot comprehend,
but feels the voice as blood in its ears, the fury, laughter, rhythm, rhyme,

and my heart strings sing,
to the call of migration,
and try to fly to a homeland
which I have never seen.

Three Rivers

Ellen McAteer

The sun momentarily turns
Rose Street gold
and makes a yellow brick road
to the river that shouts loudest.

Along that stately river
cranes lift their skeleton necks
in dinosaur dreams;
polluted beauty screams a sunset;
the sky bubbles like a kettle,
purple boiling away to cobalt,
the water, black as pig iron,
is smelted to gold.

I travel a graffitied road
under the weight of water.

Walking through Elder Park
I watch the glitter of dew on the grass
turn to the sparkle of glass on the pavement.

The sun shines in my eyes
morning and evening
when it shines at all
it shines on the new builds and the wrecking ball
it hides the police tape till I almost walk into it.
Govan, glitter and doom, burning itself to pieces:
but full of friends and neighbourly folk
tiny diamonds

made and unmade in an instant
inside the flame.

A gathering of seagulls explodes
like a snapped sheet:
storm at sea.

I take the Govan ferry back across
to the foot of the wildest river
which my dreams wander up
and down. This river drags
a rural valley
with it almost to the Clyde
and primal woods grace
its snowmelt racing in between
West End tenements and railway bridges.

To follow the Kelvin
is to walk the channels
of the mind, its rich mud
its ivy-shaded spaces
its broken millwheels
and blood-dark waterfalls
and occasionally
catch the fish of a thought
or the boot of a memory.

Many greater minds
have followed this river's pattern;
one even took it
for his name.

I cross the Clyde again
to tend to my uncle;

stop to buy vodka
his medicine of choice
at a shop backing on to
the third, secret river
which keeks between buildings,
its sister's dark reflection.

The River Cart runs
past the place where my father
lies in cold clay sleep
under a black stone
too near his so-called home.

Wherrayu FAE?
Ah canny onnerstaun yer axsent.
I am the foreigner
Wherever I go
Wot's that lilt?
U awstralian?
I was born an alien
in a city of immigrants
and brought up in city of divides
Phwat football team do you support?
I am of no religion.

My voice is like the blur of
green seen from a rushing river
a flicker of fields and hills, rising up
into concrete mountains and valleys, sometimes
crashing sea-like against something hard,
but never still, and home is a raft
moving fast, with too much luggage.

Like me, this river churns

against indifferent backs of houses
tumbles, shocked, from a country park
where trees comb its thoughts
into the sluice of Pollok,
carrying bottles and other shame
in its confused wandering under
concrete shopping-centres and motorways,
and also greets the Clyde, surprised,
from between two warehouse cliffs.

Fifty years ago, these rivers were dead:
chemical drains, poisoned by people
alive only with traffic, arterial roads;
today, the salmon swims up the Kelvin,
seals visit the city by way of the Clyde
and otters burrow in the bright Cart's banks

today, after nearly forty years
of poison, I walk the rivers of my city
and find a home within, flowering, clean, alive again,
from the falling rain, and being loved, and left alone.

The River Clyde is the main river in Glasgow, and site of most of its industry. Its name derives from the Scots Gaelic for "heard from afar". The famous physicist William Thomson, 1st Baron Kelvin was named Baron Kelvin in honour of his achievements, after the river that flowed past his university. The River Cart is formed by the meeting of the Black Cart and the White Cart tributaries; the latter flows through Pollok Park, Pollok and Shawlands. Its name possibly derives from Old Irish Gaelic cartaim, 'I cleanse'.

A Mermaid in the Clyde

Emma Wilson

Once upon a time, a mermaid was found in the Clyde.

The news flowed through the streets, flushing out the conspirators, the realists and the fanatics. She was found just before daybreak, and by 7.40am a Crowd had gathered at the mouth of the Tradeston Bridge despite the brittle pink sky that refused to melt the ice glazed over the city. The Crowd became a collective unit, and relatively productive in its curiosity. The Crowd's breath rose like steam from a factory chimney as gossip and tidbits of information were manufactured for the public interest.

A blockade of official looking people with closed faces cordoned off the area, some silent except for the low buzz and squabble of their radios, others barking orders and threats, to stay back, keep back, no comment. None was needed.

Behind the yellow tape and uniformed bodies, glimpses could be made of the water surrounding the abutment, and the figure that was caught between the rivers powerful drag and the stationary bridge support. A body, it seemed, face down towards the river bed, its upper half bobbing against the construction as its lower half flickered in and out of sight. The Crowd pieced the image together. As they absorbed what was before them, a swift silence descended and a shared fear that was hard to verbalise grew within the Crowd. Perhaps it was the possibility that this event would change everything. Her existence would change everything forever.

Long dark hair, tangled and billowing; blue-grey skin, exposed and stretched across the back –

And a tail. A fin. Scales. The Crowd erupted.

Long into the day the police worked on and under the bridge, moving the body onto a rescue boat and collecting samples from the surrounding area. More people arrived, some professionally interested, hoping for forty plus lines on the phenomenal story. One had already decided to title it 'A Tall

Tail'. Journalists tried to find the first witness for a quote, but they had been whisked away. Taken in for questioning or for shock perhaps, the Crowd said. The religious fanatic who normally inhabited Buchanan Street moved down to the riverside, pleased with this new source of doom. 'THE END OF THE WORLD' was scrawled across his strap-on poster board. Twitter vultures pecked at the leaked images and spread its carcass around the earth. Glasgow, mermaid mythology and government conspiracies made the top ten Google searches for the day. The Scottish tourist board was inundated with calls; a line of Glasgae Girl merchandise with a mermaid motif was mocked up.

In one day, everything changed. But it didn't last.

The police released a statement declaring the incident as a tragic accident, explaining that the body was that of twenty-one year old Susan Donald, a student at the Glasgow School of Art. She was a determined protestor against nuclear power and had attempted to tie herself to the Tradeston Bridge at around 5.30am. She had designed a mermaid's tail from a canvas sheet, paper mache and glitter glue, and duck taped it to her hips. Across her bare chest and stomach she had written NO NUCLEAR POWER ON OOR RIVER, hoping that the spectacle would bring new awareness to the cause. It was below zero however, and the cold caused severe hypothermia. She fell into the river below before she had properly secured herself to the railing. She was dead within minutes. The family received condolences and a body to bury and the world kept tumbling on and on.

Just as well. Reality and fantasy cannot mesh, not if there's hope of a principled, logical society being maintained (I bet they said). The grief of the girl's parents, once they had been informed, was tangible and logical. It was digestible (not for them). The discovery of a mythological creature could never have been accepted. The police report caused the hysteria to break, and so instead of a mermaid statue in the middle of George Square (expensive), there was simply a dozen bunches of flowers attached to the Tradeston Bridge as memorial of the day that everything nearly changed. An acceptable price.

Half a hand and a thumb deep

Scott McGowan

The surface and angle is found from touch. A line drawn inside the head and held in its space. Virtually held for further exploration and touch until successive lines are maintained. And held. The volume is identified. A virtual scan. Thumb to top to protect from strike. Head to side to line up with the virtual, scanned space.

Flat, flat, flat. Flat flat flat. Flat flat flat. Flat flat flat.
Flat, flat, flat.Flat flat flat. Flat flat flat.
Flat, flat, flat.
Flat, flat, flat. Flat line. Flat line. Follow the flat line. Flat line. Push the flat line along.
Define the space with a perpendicular. Flat, flat, flat. Flat, flat, flat.
Tip tap flat. Flat flat flat.
Tip tap flat.Flat flat flat. Flat flat flat.
Tip tap flat.

The point cracks towards the line, gently tipping and releasing towards the line. The field is safe.

This is the point.

Furrow towards flat. Furrow towards flat. Furrow towards the flat.

Furrow towards flat. Furrow towards flat. Furrow towards the flat.

Furrow towards flat. Furrow towards flat.   and fall.

Furrow towards flat. Furrow towards flat.   and fall.

Furrow towards flat. Furrow towards flat.   and fall.
Furrow towards flat. Furrow towards flat.   and fall.

Tipple tap furrow towrds the flat   and fall. Tipple tap topple
tip tapple   and fall. Tipple tap tap   and fall.Tipple tip tipple
    and fall. To test if the tipple tap tipple tap is true
wait for the fall. Continue the tipple tap tupple. And wait. For the fall.
Listen for the fall. Safe.

This is safe. This is the time of the claw. The claw is free.
Takes up the furrow. Lines the furrow and carries the field.
The big toop toop of the claw. Toop toop fall. Toop toop   fall.

Toop toop fall. Toop toop fall. Top toop fall. Toop toop toop
fall   and fall. Toop toop   fall   and fall. Toop
and fall.
Toop and fall. Toop toop and fall. Toop toop toop toop.   Falls

and fall   Toop   and fall.   Toop toop toop   Falls.
Fall. Toop toop   and fall. Toop toop toop toop and fall. Toop
toop toop and fall. Toop and fall. The field is lined. Toop toop fall.

Touch. The sharpness reveals the line. Return to the flat. The flat insists on the line. Tim tim tibble. Line. Tibble tibble tibble. The angle resists the flat. The cliff resists the flat. Soon the cliff is safe. (The flat insists) Soon it is safe. The vulnerable places await the point.

It's a safe point. The cliff is steep and smooth. Point along the claw. Furrow towards the cliff. Little trenches towards the cliff. Revealing little ridges, some of them are easy towards the cliff. Tipple tap tipple. Leave you. Get you. Tipple tip tapple the lines are drawn. All towards the cliff. Defensive lines are made. All in lines towards the cliff. Waiting. Tipple tip fall. Waiting for the fall....All are revealed. Unprotected.

The settlements were securely sheltered and recently protected by the ridge.

Made from stone and established here since the beginning. It's kind of a frontier settlement. The various structures tightly imbedded in the sheltered plain. There is a uniformity to the homes. The strength of the place, since the beginning, has always been in their isolation and in the way individual homes have relied on the protection of their neighbour on all sides. The beauty, and now the sadness, of the settlement is that they have always been here. Since the beginning. Snug in their obscurity and protected by those above. Recently the cliff has offered protection. The cliff has been establishing itself towards three sides of the settlement. It appears higher and steeper than in recent times. (It wasn't even there in the beginning) the settlement's population is in decline. While before, the neighbouring homes sheltered each other, they have now become far more exposed. Some have already left. The strength of the place had always been in its density. A single united frontage. A mix of an endless variety that had been arriving since the beginning and settling together in a densely layered space. Over time, the layers became invisible as one combined mass. Settlement straddled settlement as they huddled securely together. Each home or structure holds on to protect those directly adjacent.

The claw is safe. Toom toom toom and falls. Fall. Fall. The settlements resist until picked off one by one or in rows. Sometimes a structure is able to resist. Hanging on by its foundation (and supported from within. From the beginning) There is a sadness and desperation to it as it too falls to the inevitable toop toom toom of the claw. And falls. Structures fly into the air and clatter in the distance. And fall Toop toom toom. And fall. One or two desperately fly towards the claw but to no avail. There is no escape. The claw is merciless. The Settlement is cleared. A rugged bare space is left. The tops of further settlements are revealed. Exposed. This is the point.

Early Showing

George Craig

So I get to the cinema and I say, One for Corpse Bride and give her a tenner. But she doesn't take it. She looks at me, down at my legs and says, One and a half? I grin back, that sorry-for-you grin you put on when someone makes a mistake. No just the one please. Where's your child? she asks and I laugh, not laughing at her or anything, just laugh, cause you do. But now SalesAssistant-Amanda is staring at me like I'm deranged. So I set her straight, I don't have any children.

I'm sorry, Sir, she says. And I'm thinking why is she sorry that I don't have kids, didn't have a high enough sperm-count, couldn't stop Sarah getting pregnant to the bastard kitchen-fitter, in and out in three days and took the client with him. And SalesAssistant-Amanda doesn't look sorry. Her brow hunkers down. A smug pencilled-in smile snakes across her lips. She says, This is a parent and child screening. And I think Jeezus. I mean, what's the score, bringing kiddies to a grown-up movie? Fair enough if it's Bambi, all that circle of life stuff. But this is Corpse Bride. It's not cutesy. It's not sweet. It might be animated, sort of, but not one for the weans.

I let out a sigh, think about leaving. But it's the last showing in their Tim Burton season. I shrug my shoulders and say, Okay, just give me a seat near the back, away from the kids, that'll do. Her face opens, like an unclenched fist, but not relaxed, not friendly. She moves a full step to the side to look over my shoulder and I say, Hey, I get there might be some noise, but I'll take a ticket anyway.

She steps back with the hands on the hips, sinks her scowl into her triple chin, shakes her head and gives it, I'm sorry, Sir but we have to provide a safe environment for the children. And I think what's that all about? Then I get it. But she makes sure, just in case, because she's getting into a flow. She comes out with all that, Wouldn't be appropriate, Have to think of the children's welfare stuff and that word – safety, Safety, SAFETY! And in my head I'm saying, Wait a minute, are you saying that I'm not safe to be around kiddies? And in my head I'm saying, Slap her, she deserves a slap. And if I was a braver man I would. I'd extend my arm to the side of her face and graze her cheeks, one after the other, like someone in a Pushkin story, demanding satisfaction, restoring my honour. Only, I can't. Because I'm from a different generation to her; I play by different rules and she knows it. I stare at her and say nothing. She raises her eyebrows and smiles.

Suddenly, there are folk all around me. Two women buying popcorn at the confectionery counter stop mid-purchase to get an eyeful. The lady beside the velvet-roped threshold into the screens has stepped forward out of her area. I can feel the mammies and nannies behind me in the queue staring into the back of my reddening neck, mumbling, mumping their gums. I turn. Lips purse, arms fold and I'm getting stared-out. Then I realise, they're all women; women and weans. The whole cinema, the whole complex – what's with that? So I'm guilty, aren't I? The sisters can smell a bloke near children and want blood.

But I really want to see this movie, watch the Tim-boy doing his stuff. Seven weeks I've had the workmen in the flat; acro props keeping up the ceiling, front door open to the world, no electric, no gas, water on and off like a belisha beacon. And every time I've gone to see Tim B it's been, Oh we need access Mr McV or, Oh we have to work late again tonight Mr McV, or some other nonsense. I wouldn't mind if it was my fault, but it isn't. That DIY eejit upstairs with his slate floors and marble worktops and limestone walk-in shower – of course the building couldn't hold it. But none of this affects him. It's my cornice that's cracking, my walls that are starting to bow with the weight of his Barney Rubble renovations. He'll have seen the movie and at a more sociable time too, not sneaking out mid-morning behind workies' backs to be subjected to this. And I think, enough's enough. I've had it with all the cheating girlfriend, prick of a neighbour, incompetent builder, sour-faced SalesAssistant-Amanda shite. I deserve to see this movie. So I turn back round to get into it with her. I think screw you, and screw the right-onsters queuing behind me, and the popcorn guzzlers gawking on, I'm getting this sorted, here, now.

I say, What gives you the right to decide I'm not safe to be around children? She looks at me, but kind of through me. Her voice goes monotone and her eyes roll up and to the side. She says, We have a duty to provide safe surrounds for the children. Safe surrounds, honestly. I let rip at her this time, How am I making the surrounds unsafe? I'm not kicking the walls in, bringing the roof down, pissin on the seats. All I want to do is watch a movie.

I consider for a moment that I've put my point across rather well, have gained the upper hand over SalesAssistant-Amanda. She's staring at me, slack-jawed. Then I realise that I've been banging my fist, fascist-style on the counter. My little paper bag of six Satsumas bought especially for the film has dissolved into an orange mush. I feel the sticky mess of citrus juice congeal between my fingers like webbing.

She says nothing, steps back and folds her arms. The muttering starts behind me again. I try to tough it out, but can't help looking at the splatter of fruit. I don't have a tissue. Sarah always said a gentleman carries a hankie and a lighter, not for himself, but to be gallant to others. But I never carry either and I can't ask SalesAssistant-Amanda for a towel. I pull my sweatshirt sleeves down below my hands, push up the arms of my coat and begin soaking up the amber juice with my forearms, scooping segments and strips of membrane into little piles on top of the burst peel.

And she's loving it. She takes a step back and leans on one heel, like a bike on a stand. She lets me discolour both sleeves from beige to dull orange, doesn't offer me a bin for the remnants of fruit, watches me put two handfuls of Satsuma pulp into my jacket pockets. Then she gives it, I think you should leave now, Sir. I lower my head and consider my options. The pubs open in an hour. I could go home, get cleaned up, go for a pint; try to just forget it. But she jumps in again, can't resist it, says, We can't let anyone into the cinema who might pose a threat to children. Well, I can't walk away now, can I? If I walk away now, I'm some pervert who's been exposed by the toddler police. So I do the only thing I can. I pull my sleeves back under the arms of my jacket, push my chin into the air and demand, very calmly, very politely, to see the manager. Because everyone knows that only the righteous would take it to the management. Only an innocent man would raise the stakes that way.

And it works. The guzzlers leave the counter and offer ticket stubs to the attendant. The mammies and nannies behind me hush up. I look round, nod reassuringly towards them, spread my sticky palms in a downward motion to show them all's well, that the matter is being referred to a higher authority.

Some of them nod back, smile nervously, a sure sign that I'm winning. Until SalesAssistant-Amanda announces that she's the manager. I snort and point to the evidence on her wee plastic badge, the Amanda bit stuck on with print-out tape. But it turns out she is the manager, acting manager, in charge for the week while Miss Barnes takes her annual break. And that's me blown. I want a complaint form, I say and she gives me one. I want your full name, I say, even though what's there on the plastic tape is probably enough and she gives me her name too. Then I leave, because there's nothing left for me to ask her for. I turn, my face glowing, and edge along the line. I squeeze around staring toddlers being pulled closer into mums' legs. I negotiate my way past buggies with pneumatic tyres and suspension chassis. I know that I need to do something, so I look back and shout, This is discrimination, even though the word doesn't sound right in my mouth. No-one answers. I push open the plate glass door and walk away.

But on the way home I think about it, about nothing else; it's discrimination against the childless. They couldn't put up a sign saying No Women, No Asians, No Catholics, could they? It's racist. It's bigoted. It's bloody discrimination. By the time I get home, I know I'm in the right, that it was the mess of those Satsumas that made me doubt it in the moment. I spend two hours writing my letter, filling in my complaint form, preparing my case; trading standards, defamation, the works. I walk to the post box, realise as the letter leaves my hand and slips into the box, that the movie ended more than an hour ago.

I wait. You might be thinking, well that'd be that, but not for me. I make repeated phone calls to customer services, to head office. Three weeks later I get a reply, an apology and a free pass to the cinema. I tear up the free ticket and post it back to them. My second letter is longer than my first because I've educated myself in the meantime; can reference legislation, quote section numbers, threaten newspaper interest. A full seven weeks after Corpse Bride has left town, I get a letter from Head of Marketing, a director of the company. And he's absolutely in agreement with me. He's reviewing their policies, reconsidering their advertisements, changing the management. It's his pleasure to offer me a year's free pass for two into the cinema, and a complimentary meal at the sister restaurant next door, wine included.

And I think, Justice. That's something, isn't it? I mean a victory for the ordinary man; the nobody. And I think about SalesAssistant-Amanda's twisted face and walking back in there with my head held high. I'll invite the girl from 4b who moved in last month; tell her it's a 'welcome to the building' dinner, no expense spared, let her pick the feature she fancies, an early showing, and promise her a nice meal afterwards. I'll iron a sharp crease into my jeans, and I won't mention Sarah once. We'll walk in, victorious, me clutching the book of free tickets with my name embossed on the front in gold letters. Everything back as it should be; better Nichol, even.

Then a cold thought crosses me, and I realise that it'll never happen, none of it. No hand holding with 4b-girl, no fancy meal, no victory-march into the picture house. Because as soon as I do any of it, as soon as I turn up for my free meal or my free movie they'll all know. They'll know and they'll say, That's the paedo guy who tried to get in with the kiddies. And all the heads will turn again. So I'm thinking now that I'll stay home, stick to DVDs.

Early November

Jordan Mulligan

I enjoy the park at night.
In early November. Not dark
mind. Glasgow's white light
buzz flowing through trees.
Me. Ears alert to every alien
sound. The scrape of dogs' claws.
Tarmac. Grass. Tarmac.
It's whole geography in the
click of those eroding
calcium pen nibs.

An approaching red signal
breaks the mist. Appear then
gone. Repeat and repeat. The not
quite smooth transitions of tooth.
    and chain.
the grit pressured. Sighing into
dust under this form of light
and sound's path which
stretches past
us.

The tribal calls of invisible
groups. Tear violently
through still air.
A glance over the shoulder.
An audible flame in the
distance. Beaten chests and
outrageous foreign cries.

A living fantasy in the
distant unseen elsewhere.
The University, a Neo-Gothic
Funeral pyre. Glowing.
Creeping into view.
erect and sexless.

I hear a pop in the distance.
Watch the flowering lights
of distant firework displays.
My mind fixes on them
thrown towards me.
Revels in it.
Imagine it:
Splitting the fog
a sulphurous serpent
shedding flakes of
glowing skin,
casting them aside
in its constant
progress
towards me.
and I will
catch it
and wait
for the
coming
bang.

Between the Signs

extract from a novel

Deborah Andrews

The bus crawled back to Glasgow along the busy M8, but Maddie finally caught a glimpse of George Square. It was strung with Christmas lights: massive golden bells that illuminated back and forth through three stages giving the illusion they were swinging; giant leaves of holly, each with three red berries; and her favourite: 3D neon angels complete with yellow haloes. Eighty quid for the day's role-play work – as soon as the cheque arrived, she'd go straight to the pawnbrokers, get her dad's wedding ring back. And there'd still be enough left over for some food and a piece of blow.

Unusually, Glasgow felt colder than Edinburgh, but after the stifling journey the fresh air was a relief. From a phone box in the bus station she called the flat again: still no-one home. No point rushing back to an empty pad. Buttoning up her coat, she decided to walk.

Sauchiehall Street was packed with Christmas shoppers. A duo playing a medley of Oasis songs competed with the Salvation Army's 'Hark the Herald Angels Sing', but outside M&S a small crowd had gathered. It broke into enthusiastic applause. Stretching her neck to see why, a thrill ran through her. Alex. Her instinct was to put her head down and hurry away, but she didn't.

Iggy was right: Alex rode well. His feet cycled back and forth through 180° enabling him to balance as, with utter concentration, he juggled what looked like five snowballs. Turning a full circle, he tossed three of them to a group of kids. The fourth he splattered against one of the fathers' chests, feigning an exaggerated apology as the kids giggled wildly. Then he spotted Maddie, smiled and broke the fifth in two. In its centre was the head of a rose. He leant back and landed on his feet, catching his unicycle by its post. Bowing, he presented her with the flower, but, as she reached to take it, the petals transformed into a butterfly that fluttered rapid spirals up into the night sky.

Maddie laughed and the crowd cheered. Alex grabbed her hand and pulled her into the circle, raising her arm and having her bow too, as if they'd been a double act.

One of the mums ushered her daughter forward to put some money in his pirate hat, and another couple of the kids came to stare at the unicycle.

'How long have you had the bike?' the snowballed man asked.

'My dad took us to the circus when I was eight; I pestered for one after that, got one for my birthday. This fella I saved up for and bought about six years ago.'

'Impressive act.'

'Thanks.' Alex gestured to the man's jacket, 'Sorry about the attack.'

'He got you, daddy!' A wee boy wrestled the man's legs and was hoisted up onto his shoulders.

'Certainly did!' The man counted out some change and dropped it into the hat. 'Get yourself and the lady a drink.'

Maddie flushed – did they look like a couple?

As the crowd dispersed, Alex turned to her. 'Can I buy my fair assistant a beverage?'

'I didn't do anything!'

'Au contraire!' He collapsed the unicycle, tipped the coins into a small cloth bag, then landed the pirate hat on her head.

No make-up, a day of crying; now sporting a pirate hat – surely not a good look...

'Besides,' he said, pulling on his jacket, 'it was a condition of the donation.'

She glanced at the phone boxes, would Mike be home yet?

Alex wrapped a houndstooth scarf round his neck.

'It wasn't a real butterfly, was it? How would it survive?'

The corner of his mouth quivered. 'Come for a drink and I might tell you.' He ran his fingers through his hair but his fringe fell back over his brow.

Ridiculous to be so nervous, how would she ever manage a conversation? She slid the hat from her head, but he linked his arm through hers.

'I'll take that as a yes then!'

They came out of Nico's about half nine. A group of women sashayed past singing, 'Ole ole, ole ole!'

'See,' Alex pointed to the ground, 'there's some of those flowers I was telling you about.'

Beneath a grid of glass cobbles, the heads of what looked like chrysanthemums were set against coloured backgrounds and lit from beneath.

Maddie leant forward. 'I'd not noticed them before.'

'They're fairly recent. Part of an environmental art project.'

'But the glass paving's always been there?'

'Yeah. At least, since Victorian times. They used to let daylight into cellars and shop basements.'

'The things you don't know... Which reminds me! What about that butterfly?'

'Ah...' he seemed to consider it, 'let's just say it's one of life's mysteries.'

'Oh, come on! What about the snowballs then, what were they made of?'

'Hmmm. The nature of mysteries... I mean like now – life expects us to walk to Charing Cross and say goodbye and that's that, right? But what if we turned round and walked this street again – would we upend life's plan, or would that be *part* of its plan?'

'You're assuming life has a plan.'

'A libertarian?'

'Maybe. Just seems an awful lot of us to each have an individual fate.'

'But we don't know for sure, right? It's a mystery. Don't you look up at the stars sometimes and feel almost decimated with awe?'

'Like a coconut?'

He peered down at her with a playful stern stare. '*Decimated...*'

'Sorry. You were saying...?'

'D'you ever get an overwhelming fizzy feeling that you have to, like, just run off?'

'I can't say that's something I can really relate to.'

He laughed.

At the street corner a man was selling copies of *The Big Issue*. Alex took a couple of quid from his cloth bag.

'Help the homeless, mate?'

'Cheers. Keep the change.' Folding the magazine, Alex tucked it in his jacket pocket. 'Actually, are you going to be here for the next ten minutes or so?'

The man sipped from a polystyrene cup. 'Aye. Why'd you ask?'

'Could you keep an eye on the bike for me?' Alex propped it up beside the cash point.

'No problem,' the man shrugged.

Securing his hat on his head, Alex cocked an eyebrow. 'Last one back to the Christmas tree's a numpty!'

Maddie watched him run. In her head she heard Roger declare that the position of numpty seemed to have already been filled. She laughed then set off after him, weaving between people coming out of pubs and couples perusing restaurant menus. The cold night air rushed against her face and the world shone.

Just past Bradford's she called, 'Alex! Hey, Alex!'

He turned.

Pointing down, she asked, 'Is this part of that environmental art project?'

He made his way back towards her, peering at the pavement. When he was close enough to touch, she took off, sprinting past him.

'Hey!'

She was within reach of the Christmas tree when he grabbed her round the waist, picked her up and spun her round. 'A cheat! A total cheat!'

'A numpty! A total numpty!' She laughed, panting clouds of breath.

Setting her down, he turned her round then led her in stumbling circles that became a polka, singing, 'Oh Christmas tree, oh Christmas tree, of all the trees most lovely…'

Behind him, the world was a blur of people in hats and scarves and the arms of the fir tree laced with coloured bulbs.

When they stopped, the world seemed to keep on spinning.

'Look, angels are having a pillow fight …

Following his gaze, she saw soft feathers of snow drifting down to them out of a sodium sky. He still had hold of her hand. In a rush of awkwardness she crouched down, pretending her laces needed re-tied.

All the way back down Sauchiehall Street she could feel how his hand had held hers – its heat, width, slightly rougher skin: artist's hands. He'd said he'd liked sculpture best at art school, and hoped to get back to it soon. 'But it's hard. Sometimes I feel like there's sixty lives I want to lead. How am I supposed to pick just one?'

At the street corner, a small group of guys had gathered. One of them was propped between two friends, holding onto their shoulders as he tried to balance on the unicycle. The wheel slipped beneath him and he was catapulted forwards, only just finding his feet. The unicycle bounced on the ground.

'Sorry,' the Big Issue seller pointed with his thumb, 'couldn't keep them off it.'

'Oi, Calico Jack!' one of the guys called. 'Is this yours?'

'Yep.'

'Bloody impossible!'

'Takes practice.'

'Let's see then.'

'Nah, I'm done for tonight.'

'Come on, man! Just a wee turn!'

Alex stepped on a pedal and, like an obedient witch's broom, the unicycle sprang up under him.

'No way, man!'

He balanced along the kerb, hopped off, cycled back and forth then span three times like an ice-skater.

The guys clapped. 'Hats off to Calico Jack!'

'Hey!' one of them called, 'why are pirates pirates?'

'Cos they arrrr!' the others replied, grabbing their friend round the neck and ruffling his hair.

'Do you get that a lot?' Maddie asked as they walked on.

'I don't mind when it's friendly.' He stopped outside the Canton Express. 'Noodles?'

If she'd had any money left… 'I better be getting back. It's been a long day.'

'Can I walk you?'

'It's okay. I'm used to getting about by myself.' A twinge of guilt: she'd not mentioned Mike. Please god they wouldn't bump into him, rolling out of somewhere, steaming.

'D'you know it's a gibbous moon tonight. If we could see it… Well, it *is* a gibbous moon. Whether we can see it or not is incidental.'

'A gibbon moon?!'

'Gibb*ous*! *Gibbous…*'

'Stop monkeying around.'

'Oh, ah ha ha. Look it up!'

'No such word.'

'A pound says I'm right.'

'Deal!'

They shook on it. For a moment, her hand back in his.

The corners of his mouth curled. He doffed his hat and bowed. 'I look forward to collecting my pound!'

As she headed west, away from the city centre, the sky lost its orange glow, becoming blacker. Stars appeared. 'Gibbous moon…' She laughed. Beneath the street lamps the snow sparkled like glitter.

Looking up at the unlit windows of her flat, she almost didn't want to go in. Alex would be arriving back at Sam's about now. There'd probably be a group there, sitting around, telling jokes and stories.

In the hall, the answering machine was flashing – five messages. She pressed play. The first was for Callum; the second, the one she'd left for Mike from Edinburgh; the third, her mum, again; next, Mike slurring something about being home soon; and, lastly, a voice that was initially unfamiliar.

'Hello. This is a message for Madeline. I just wanted to let you know I've had some excellent feedback from Ian about your work today. It was a pleasure meeting you, and I hope you'll come and work with us again. I'll certainly be in touch when something suitable next comes up. In the meantime, wishing you the very best with all your endeavours.'

She listened to the message again, then stood in her bedroom in the dark, looking out. Flinging up the window she was met with a fresh chill and the sound of distant traffic. The snow was falling more thickly now and the roofs leading back to the city centre were already laced white. *Excellent feedback… more work in the future…* Something bubbled up in her, that fizzy feeling Alex described, and she *did* want to run, out over the rooftops, run and run and run until her feet hardly touched the tiles and she started floating up – up and up and up, twisting and turning as snowflakes melted on her hands and face.

Then she remembered: she was keen to get a look in the dictionary.

Something old, something new, something borrowed ... happiness

The children of Dalmarnock Primary all sitting at assembly wearing uniform on a Monday morning.

baby boy

It was azure fading to turquoise as it reached the horizon.

It reminds me of ICE

Escaping the grey, visiting the exotic.

Muddy, Buddy or B.B. Choose your Guitar God!

The colour of the sky and sea from which came light and life in Godde's continuing creation.

Playing on the beaches when I was younger.

The light that brings safety and comfort in the darkest times

A brisk stroll on a cloudless winters starry night in Ardnamurchan with the full moon as our torchlight

I think it is a cold colour not warm

The colour of tanned hides before being dyed to the customers shade

There's something about watching your Nan get her hair done ... something between admiration and bemusement!

The greyhound is my favourite breed of dog. Turns out they're not grey though — bit of a blow.

Oh, those eyes, so deep-sparkling in sunlight, dreamy and haunting, angry and passionate innocent... loved.

As a colour it varies as emotion Its Sad, it identifies friend and foe yet surrounds us all

A depth as deep as an ocean and a range as far reaching as a desert sky.

Is an effect of light with a wavelength between 450 and 500nm.

old, neglected, forgotten .. transformed .. rejuvenated, reinvigorated. redefined.

appears cooler when next to orange and warmer when next to green, brings trust, peace and order.

The saltire swirls in the wind as Wallace declared victory and freedom for the Scots.

Time and tide wait for no man

Peace and tranquility, waves pounding on rocks, Ullapool, next stop America.

Meadow of dainty forget-me-nots dancing in the breeze.

When the wheels are locked there is no red in the sky.
Conjures to me a relaxed, embracing cocoon in which (although dangerous) I feel safe; in control and ultimately alive.
In daybreak's first light Vulcan began to blow a new wind of change.
America Sky's and white picket fences
Crystal clear insight sparking creativity & innovation
Life is so colourful no depression, sharing love, friendship, peace, joy, sunshine and flowers in our Bridgeton Community.
the colour makes me think of eyes
COLD WAVES CRASHING ON A CRYSTAL CLEAR DAY
Speed = Frequency × Wavelength. Speed = $4{\cdot}75\times10^{-7}$ meters × $6{\cdot}67\times10^{14}$ Hertz = $3{\cdot}05\times10^{8}$ meters per second
It makes me think of nature, space, power, depth ...... ROY G BIV .... and my wife's eyes
Faith is looking to the skies, the heavens, gentle fragile souls seeking light, hope, peace and love.
Tranquil moments inspire me to explore my hidden depths and gives me hope for the future.
010000100100110001010101010000101
The sound of my son's laughter.
Ocean meeting sky. Sky over you, beyond you. Sea at your feet drawing you in.
.... add a ray of sunshine a drop of water and then you have Green.
Clean, fresh and cold but the bells on the forest floor are a sign of summer.
Feeling calm and peaceful lying in a state of tranquility as I drift off to sleep
The Snow Queen's dress is a perfect example sharp frosty and cold with lots of sparkle.
Kid I don't know much about you, but I like you, cause you're true....
THE HOTTER INNER PORTION of THE FLAME CONTRASTS WITH THE OUTER RIM of YELLOW.
The sky on a crisp autumn day contrasting with the warm colours on the trees and the smell of decaying leaves in the air
forget about your worries and strife ALL you need is the bare necessities of life.
The Donegal sea became a deep ultramarine, set against an indigo sky ablaze with stars, almost close enough to touch.
When I look in my wardrobe and see my shirts and all the different shades.

It's more than a state of mind, its a calm serene feeling that makes me happy and safe.

Sadness, despair, pride, hope and awe mixed with a touch of fear and a mother's unconditional love for her son.

A fine and subtle spirit dwells in every little flower...

Beneath A GREAT SKY, SHROUDED IN TEAL-GREY MIST A PROCESSION OF WOAD PAINTED CELTS TREAD SOFTLY BY.

When growing up it reminded me of the Police.

Blisteringly hot or searingly cold and the same as Sinatra's peepers'

Can be Calming

This colour reminds me of my Eyes

I do have clothes of other colours but...

Calm waves sweep across deep Seas and if the wind is right you can Sail away to Serenity.

Growing up beneath the warmth and brightness which makes things appear vivid and clear.

The view of where I want to be...

I Can't wait to hear the jazz man Sing!

Suddenly and unexpectedly.

It's just a colour, it doesn't have to define you

Aim for the sky and you'll reach the ceiling. Aim for the ceiling and you'll stay on the floor.

The Ocean: Tsunami, Greenpeace, Over Fishing, Climate Change, War, Shark Attack, Oil Spillage, Whale Hunting, Renewable Energy, Piracy.

In god eyes Everone is Beautiful Loving Understanding Equal we are all god children

Stars shining in the desert night, Kings travelling on into the light.

my daughter abbys Favourite colour bright and bold JUST like my daughter

Low quiet words of love in my ears now and again, golden, elegant and strange, like seahorses, like grace notes, tiny floating saxophones.

THE COLOUR OF A SAIL AND COULD BE THE COLOUR OF A WHALE

Looking up, crisp white lines draw a saltire on a boundless canvas; a special day lies ahead.

Beautiful, Solid, clear and calm

As a young boy the pictures from space filled me with wonderment Red, yellow, grey the planets Came alive in my mind The most beautiful was Earth, my home.

Reminds me of People being upset

ANOTHER RAINY SUNDAY AFTERNOON: NO ONE TO TALK TO, NOTHING TO DO.

It's the darkness of night that covers the land, the she-cats eye as she hunts for her prey, disturbing the midnight silence.

gold. and silver and brass and purple. and scarlet. and fine linen and goats hair

THE COLOUR OF THE SKY IS THE COLOUR OF my EYES

Nineteen seventy-nine, the colour of shadow on snow, Brian, the colour of shadow on, snow.

The Parker, Montblanc Meisterstuck, Sheaffer Snorkel, Pelikan, Eversharp Skyline and Heaneys Conway Stewart.

All I want is my glad eye to catch a glint in your Northern flinty face again just once

The natural flag fluttering confidently in the wind on a clear, cold day.

IT'S ASSOCIATED WITH. DEPTH. STABILLITY, PEACE. SERENITY, TRANQUILITY, FAITH, TRUTH, HEAVEN.

I like it complicated like petrol

Calmness and serenity. A sea to wash away uncertainties.

Time on my hands could be time spent with you...

THROUGH PICASSOS PERIOD, THE MUSICAL NILE, LORD. SCOTTISH SKY, WARM FRENCH SEA, AND MY FAVOURITE TEESHIRT.

Something old, something new, something borrowed, something ...

Heart and soul, colour washed by the women who have sung it: Mahalia, Aretha, Reese, Billie, Rosetta, Etta.

"Are we stupid or just naive to continue to believe that money can buy us anything."

Warm And Cold Happy And Sad Crisp Clinical Mellow.

Lapis Lazuli $(Na,Ca)_8(AlSiO_4)_6(S,SO_4,Cl)_{1-2}$.

If you don't know I'll give you a clue a colour to rhyme with true.

WHEN I LOOK OUT THE WINDOW AND IT'S BRIGHT, I KNOW I AM GOING TO HAVE A GOOD DAY

to some it is tribal - loved or reviled, to others it is hope - horizon and sky.

Blau: A drechit stormy nicht afore the daurkenin

---- last 1970's band - - -

My eyes were drawn to the solitary balloon as it rose slowly upwards and eventually disappeared from view.

Ephemeral

Emeline Morin

She's at the airport, looking intently at people coming and going.
She wonders how she'll remember Glasgow when she's old.

It was my last stop in Europe that summer. I had been there for four days.
I started by visiting everything that was on my guide.

The Botanic Gardens, and its impressive glasshouses and collection of tropical plants. Massive goldfish too.
The Kelvingrove Museum, Scotland's most popular free attraction.
Glasgow Cathedral and its Necropolis. A wonderfully atmospheric medieval monument.
The People's Palace. Sauchiehall Street. George Square. Art School. Mackintosh.

But that day I did not visit. I had met a man in a bar the night before.
I wondered for a while whether I should go and meet a stranger. Sober. Foreign. Slightly lost.
I had met him in Nice'n'Sleazy's and thought that it fitted him quite well too. I did not remember his name until it flashed on my phone.
I put on a red dress, matching lipstick, strappy heels and I had done my hair up.

I was not sure I would but I recognised him instantly. He brought me to the Willow Tea Rooms. I remember mentally checking it in my to do list.
We talked art and rubbish drinking tea and eating creamy strawberry tarts.
I noticed how his hands moved while he talked, how my own bracelets clinked on the table every time I reached for my cup.

He took my hand in the street; we went to a bar. We social smoked with people whose names and faces quickly became a blur.
The streets looked different. Bluish. I didn't know which part of town we were in.

We went out. Danced. Touched. Kissed.

He made me laugh. We ran through the streets. My head was spinning. I pulled him towards me when we got to the park and he pulled up my dress. We fell asleep in the grass. I woke up at dawn.
I was still drunk but cold and covered in dew.
He was still asleep.
I quickly scribbled something on a receipt left in my handbag. I had planned on keeping it for my travelling book. I can't remember what it was now. I put the note in his pocket, kissed him gently and walked back to my hotel.

The more she thinks about it the more his face fades.

She gets up and slowly walks to gate 4.

Glasgow. Nice city, not as dark as people say. They have a cute wee cathedral. Nice bars and people. I wore a low cut red dress and made fleeting love under the stars.

Flying Solo

Siobhan Staples

Up was the heartening and the strong reply.
The heart of standing is we cannot fly.

'Hello Madam.' I hold out my hand, nails fresh-slicked Frosted Rose. 'Can I see your boarding pass please?'

The woman smiles, hands me the two pieces of paper, and starts fussing over the baby, un-strapping it from the buggy, retrieving bags and toys and lidded cups from underneath. Her hair is scrunched back with a tortoiseshell clip that fails to disguise it's in need of a good wash. I don't look at the baby, but catch a smudge of pink and white so I'm guessing girl. Not that it matters.

Gate 29a, Flight BA2965, Glasgow to London Gatwick. It's a Tuesday morning, and not the holidays, but still the flight is almost full and I have ten minutes to get ninety-seven people through this door and into their seats.

The woman straightens up, holding the baby, and I know what's coming.

'Could you just take her for a moment so I can fold up the buggy?' She's still smiling, already handing the chubby, wriggling bundle towards me and expecting me to play along. And really, who can blame her? I've seen how it works with the other girls, how they squeal a delighted of course! How they coo and fuss.

'I'm afraid that's not possible, Madam.' I hold her gaze as the corners of her mouth begin to crumple. 'It's a Health and Safety policy.'

'But every time I've flown before I've– '

'Other staff may be more careless about the rules, Madam,' I cut her off with the efficient smile I use for work, 'but it is the rule, nonetheless. Now, if you'd like to tell me how to fold this up?' I turn my attention to the buggy as she moves the baby onto her hip.

'But it really is a bit of an awkward one. It'd be much easier if you'd– '

'Is it this red button first?'

'No, first you have to release these clips here…'

She's right, it is a complicated sod, and by the time I've wrestled it down ready for the hold I'm starting to sweat a little and the passengers behind her are getting restless, a navy-suited businessman muttering God's sake and totally *ridiculous,* the people around him nodding in agreement.

Maybe that's why it happens, because I'm thinking about these other passengers, focusing on keeping the mood polite and courteous. Whatever the reason, I somehow forget, and take too deep a breath.

'Are you alright?' The woman is looking at me, her eyes creased a little in concern, and I realise I'm leaning against the cabin door. I can see she's about to move in closer to me, the baby beginning to grizzle on her hip.

'I'm fine thank you, I just stood up a little too quickly.' To be honest I'm struggling to regain my poise, but I can do a passable impression. 'Would you mind taking your seat now please?'

The woman looks unsure for a moment, but then mercifully moves away, along with the pink and white bundle of danger.

I close my eyes as we start to taxi along the runway. Almost twenty years of flying and I still love this moment: the sudden thrust of speed, the jolt of leaving the ground, the sway as the plane pushes up into nothing but air. The barefaced outrageousness of it still gives me a thrill. As we tip sideways, turning south, I open my eyes. The city is spread below us like a map, from the red-roofed tower blocks of the Southside to the sharp spikes of the University spires to the green ridge of the Campsie Fells beyond, and the Clyde sludging through the heart of it all, like a furred artery. Then we level off again and all I can see is the cloud-line. This is moment I love best: the moment we are truly away.

When I first started the job it was purely about getting away from Her, and she was raging.

A trolley dolly darling? she'd hissed, giving me The Look, the one she used to turn on Daddy: big wounded eyes like a little dog that's just been kicked. It worked a treat on him, but not me. I can't stand little dogs.

Oh, Fiona. Daddy would've been so disappointed.

I let her have her moment. There was little point in trying to reason with her as the tears ran mascara streaks down her cheeks and a shaky hand poured the first glass of something soothing.

Actually I did try to explain once, a few years later. I wanted to tell her how much I loved the job, the flying, tell her how I hadn't made a mistake at all, maybe see if we could make one last attempt at... something. But I spent too long practising my little speech, pacing a furrow in the wide floorboards of the flat, and by the time I arrived at Southview Drive she couldn't even hear the doorbell. As I let myself in I knew what I'd find: her snoring on the sofa, the final glass of the evening dribbling its sticky dregs into the carpet. I gave her a shake, but she just snuffled and carried on snoring, so I threw a duvet over her and left.

I can't remember how long ago that was now. A couple of years? More than one, less than five is all I know for sure.

The first signal comes through from the pilot and I un-strap my belt. As I'm unlocking the drinks trolley I hear a clicking from the front row and have to re-lock the trolley so I can go and investigate. It's the blue-suited businessman, and he's already half-way out of his seat. By the time I persuade him to sit down again my cheeks are aching with keeping the smile in place, and the pilot has turned off the passenger seatbelt sign anyway.

I was supposed to be working the rear today, but I've persuaded Jayne to swap. I pointed out a random chubby-faced young man in Row Twenty, sitting just behind the woman and the baby, and told Jayne I recognised him as one of the nurses from my mum's ward at The Southern, and it would just be too upsetting to have to talk to him. As we start pushing the drinks trolleys up the aisle towards each other – the passengers shifting in their seats at the promising clink of bottles – Jayne glances at me and mouths okay? I smile and nod back, dropping ice cubes into a plastic glass and handing it to the businessman, along with his whisky.

The baby has begun to screech. Her ears will be popping with the air pressure, not that it's any of my concern. I've never really been the broody type, never one for leaning into prams and pulling silly faces, turning shiny-eyed. So the decision I've made hasn't been difficult. Not once I'd realised it was simply a question of responsibility.

I made the decision one morning, when I'd been sitting in the hospital all night looking at Mum's yellowed, skinny hand, listening to her raggedy breathing and thinking about how she'd sat in this same place almost thirty years before, watching her own mother slipping noisily away. She'd described it to me often enough, not particularly spared me any details, and I was sitting there trying to work out just how she could have stumbled down exactly the same path, to exactly this same fate. It made no sense. Then one of the nurses stuck her head round the door to see how things were, and to pass on a magazine she'd just finished, to help me pass the time. It was one of those trashy things I would never buy: pages of minor celebrities and grainy photos of Hollywood royalty, but I started flicking through it anyway, and that's where I found the story, about the twins.

It was one of those true life stories. These twins had been born to an alcoholic who wasn't considered fit for motherhood, rightly enough, so they'd been adopted, but separately, by families living at opposite ends of the country. Once they were grown up the twins made a few attempts to find each other, without success, until the day they walked into the same room in the same community centre for the same meeting: Alcoholics Anonymous.

It dawned on me then what my responsibility was. I've never touched a drop myself, never daft enough to think I could travel that slippery path in safety, but it seems to me that there are some things we don't choose. Some things that are simply in our blood, part of our legacy.

So I made a promise right at the end, as the last of her breath rattled in and out. *This is where it stops Mum, this particular flawed little line.* And I've never considered it a great sacrifice, to be honest. Although recently things do seem to be a little more... challenging.

It's just the smell. Like a fresh-opened jar of vanilla sugar. The first strawberries of summer. I'd be fine, if it wasn't for the smell.

'Thank you. Goodbye. Thank you. Thank you.'

I'm in my position by the cabin door as the passengers file from the plane. It's taken the woman a little longer to gather herself and the baby together and she's the last to leave, struggling down the narrow aisle with the baby on her hip and two large bags slung over her shoulder, bumping and catching on the backs of the seats as she moves towards me. I'm prepared this time, more careful.

'Are you feeling ok now?' she asks.

'Fine, thank you. Goodbye. Thank you.'

As they move away the baby turns and looks back at me, blue eyes wide.

She suddenly sticks out a chubby little hand and starts opening and closing her fat little fingers like a winking eye. They move out of sight around the corner and I'm left standing looking down the empty corridor.

Geordie Monologue

Sarah Weir

ee I can't believe I forgot to tell ya, I've just had a lot on wiv me body poppin and that! Aye I took it up on top of zumba so I can look like wor Cheryl Cole. So, our landlord turns around to me and gans I need you to move out for a month in December so I have time to finish off the rest of the house. Because let's face it, the house wasn't finished man. There was geet bits of the wall crumbling onto the floor so all these spiders and minging stuff was getting into the house. Wey, I cannit stand them me. Too creepy... Wey they've got eight eyes and legs Shelley, what do they need aal that for? Anyway, the stupid heating never worked and the bloody shower still hasn't been fixed. He gans to me last October and promised it would be finished by Halloween; and look, all the bairns are back to school – it's September Shelley! Ya kna what I mean, that's well over a year doon the line. So I'm pissed off coz I'll have to sleep on somebody's bloody floor or summit for a month over Christmas while he does aal the work. Who chucks someone outta their house at bloody Christmas? Scrange, thats who! What ya saying to iz Shells...? Aye, ya kna who Scrange is man! The proper tight git who didn't give his money to anyone, from the Muppet Christmas Carol... Aye him! So anyways, that's what he tells me... He only gans and tells another lassie I'm living with that he's packing in the bloody contract! I'm like, mate, get ya story straight! So, I thought, like, I'm ganna be bloody homeless unless I find somewhere else to live. So I just get on it, ya kna what I mean? Whip me laptop oot and gans on the internet and that to find another place for me and these other lassies to stay. One comes up: spacious three bedroom maisonette it said. Wey, I didn't kna what a 'masonet' was did I? I'd never even heard of it before, I always thought it was some kind of sauce or summit. So I thought I'd gan and see it anyway. There wasn't a picture on the website or nowt but I thought I'd have some faith, believe in Jesus and aal that – but fuck me, I'll tell ya why they didn't put a bloody picture up! It was fucking minging man! They probs would have gotten mugged if they whipped a camera oot in that estate! The taxi driver didn't wanna look around at anyone in case he got jumped on! Aye, that's how bad the place was – everyone looked proper rough, even the little bairns were pure glaring! There was glass aal owa the floor, not in the windows where they're meant to live. It looked bad from the ootside like but I thought nar, I'll give it a try... I walk in and all ya can smell is fucking shite... No dead serious like Shelly. Honestly, it hit us like a tonne of bloody bricks man. I had just eaten me breakfast and I'm proper lucky it didn't come back up.It was like summit from SAW man! I thought Jigsaw was ganna come along and pure put one of those bear trap things on me head! Eee but seriously, I'm no Tulisa from N-Dubz, but I thought I was a little classier than that. There was piss on the walls and... say that again big S... nar there wasn't any skid marks man! What is it with ye and skid marks? It was a building, not a fucking toilet... you're disgusting man, Shelley! But aye, it did kinda look like a prison or summit, like the stairway was dead bare and made of that stony material. Dead cold and that. Even the estate agent looked like he was gonna shit himself. I'm surprised they didn't eat him alive like... Did I take the place? Shelley, are ye shitting me? I ran a fucking mile, I'm actually lucky to still be alive and that. So anyways, what are ya dressing up as for Christine's fancy dress party? Shut up man! Are ya honestly? I'm dressing up as a brick to get laid.

St Mungo

Mairi McCloud

'This is the bird that never flew, This is the tree that never grew, This is the bell that never rang, This is the fish that never swam.'

From your childhood,
You heard the stories of your mothers disgrace:
How one man seduced her,
And another threw her out of the house.
From your earliest moments you saw
The brutishness of man.
So when God called you to a holier life,
You were glad to go,
Knowing you would never be tempted
To handle a woman in such a way.

You did all you could to grow in gentleness,
Not minding the teasing of the other boys.
The fire that you kept burning from the hazel branch
Was but a reflection of your burning heart.
The robin which you coaxed back to life
Sang the song it learned from you.

And when Queen Lagoureth came
Pleading for her life,
Here was your chance to right the wrongs
That men did to their wives, their sisters and their daughters.
The ring, given by the queen to her knight
The ring, taken by the king from the knight
The ring you found in the belly of the salmon.
That saved this woman's life.

Where is the bell that rang in the streets
So many years ago?
Ring out the bells of Glasgow town
from Gallowgate to Castle Street.
Ring out the bells and let them join
The music of the bird-filled air.

Imogen in the Afternoon

Andrew Latimer

Not the short violent shudder
nor the long marrowless fingers
that reach into rooms to disturb
and tease, or the face that lingers

long into the night then stretched out
flat on a dry bed, fades away.
Not carrion comfort reclining
nor this procreative decay.

Imogen scratches at her sides
and curls the whole world in her hair
the mole below her hanging breast
is hanging off yet debonair.

Back in bed she prolongs the fuss
arching the back of the afternoon…
This rhythmic dance of wretched hands
Instigates our mutual rancune.

Imogen in the Evening

Andrew Latimer

Not even Circe could enchant
a host of grieving men like her,
in the taxi and in the pub
singing 'Sunken, Drunken Elpenor!'

They swapped their sobs for whisky straight
and watched her play Tiresias' part,
the creature with a sage's mind
was teaching man the art of fart.

And I have gone between the stands
within the cobbled line, walking
in the burning night, turning left
and to myself mostly talking.

Though circling, I have not descended,
but returned and recognised less
each time, and when they ask I say
'I'm not the one, that you profess'.

The pub's a fine and happy place,
where all with Imogen embrace.

sarah-ann lee, 2012

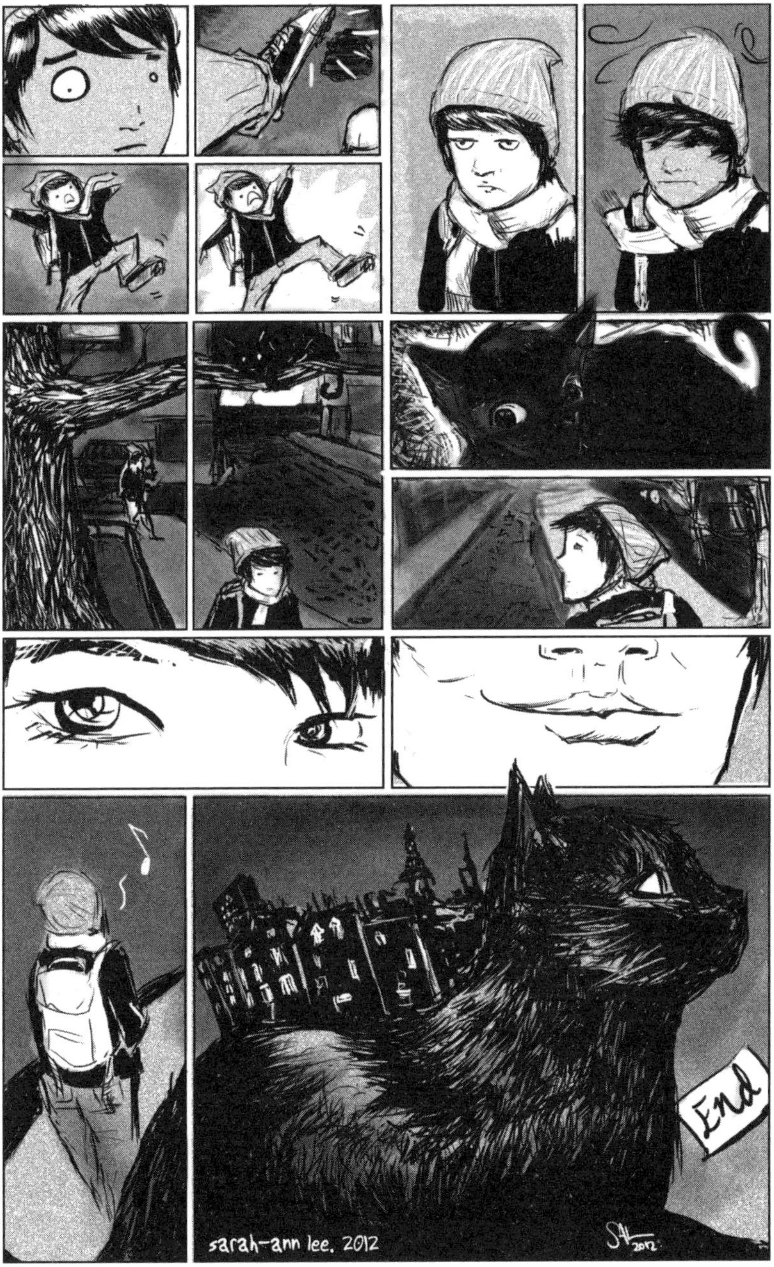
End
sarah-ann lee. 2012
SAL 2012

Sister

John Conlon

It's easy for beautiful people to be nice; just as the paper this is written on absorbs the ink, so do strangers' faces soak up their poise. When I board a bus to be greeted by a monosyllabic grunt, for him or her: they arrive and the driver is renewed, their smile, their teeth and you know the rest... I'm not bitter – I just observe. But what's the point in complaining, about as pointless as explaining that you're going on holiday to your pet. The dog, if he could understand, might care, the cat – well cats don't give a shit.

I'm one of those people who likes to step into the bathroom and look at my reflection in the mirror, as the half-light alters my hue in the soft reversal of time. When I arrived here, first I wondered what sort of place it was, whether the sun set like a tomato in hot water, whether the elements mingled magenta and cornflower blue to make the twilight the way I wanted it to be – the way I see it: its bold elusive might. Great ships do indeed require deep water and the Clyde is deep. I've thought about those ships these last few months, about the little hands, the tiny lines, the precision, the hoarse reproaches and all of this in a chorus like knife and fork. Once I'd been here a while I got to know people; one gets to know people easily here – and I heard about their lives and toil, the indignities they had suffered and the stoic nothingness of those who spend their days sat on benches, contrasted with the tale of the former boilermaker who spent his dotage on a cruise liner relay, reasoning that it was cheaper than a nursing home – and obviously the scenery was better.

Not all my friends are old, some are young – when a child looks at me what do they see? I wonder about the people I stared at as a child and do not remember – what of the feelings they felt and the fury or fear contained within stances and the turn of a head. Ten years ago when I was a child I would stare at men in bars and guess what it was they spoke of in the mystery of those paired complicities; perhaps they spoke of things like this:

Why don't we ask questions like the ones we did when we were little?

Like?

Like, where does the wind come from?

Yeah, or who invented zippers!

Listen, let's agree not to find out, the question may turn out more interesting than the answer.

Agreed?

Yep agreed.

The two had gifted themselves this day in the name of leisure, upon the grounds of a fragile awards system, the mechanics of which are familiar only to students and some civil servants. They shook hands on it and the cuff buttons on their wrists touched momentarily. The kitchen in the bar had closed, signalling the arrival of mid afternoon and the friends had been drinking since shortly before twelve; a veil of dust was visible on the mantle by the pew they occupied as the midwinter sun stole among the worn pine furniture. The boy dwelt upon time – the ticking of the time piece on his wrist and the delay in the second report from a nearby cathedral bell. He imagined the fingers touching the rope and the play of the coarse on callous amid hands unseen. The bell across the threshold and up the greasy street, the pinging till within arms reach, the looped evening sports report echoing from the bar: a Sunday evening symphony in the twenty-first century.

Pints passed, cheers followed and the two began to notice new things about each other; a heel scuffed to the left betraying a flaw in posture not discerned before, the posture of this friend, a drinking compatriot but not yet held in confidence. The boy noticed that his friend possessed grace; lustreless eyes but grace perhaps in the carriage or the palm forever framing cheek when the bar to stool height permitted. His friend in those plateaued sequences of inebriation noticed things too: the pout that always accompanied a retort, eyes spitting thoughts or a tapped foot indicating impatience to communicate a point – that delicious taste of loquacious suspension which we all know. It was good to be safe, good to be warm and good not to be alone as the evening closed upon them. It was past six now and the two relocated nearer the fire – the warmth suiting their moods towards one another – content in the realms of new discoveries accepted now as part of the person they knew better.

They were by now regulars in the bar, which is why, when they saw two girls unknown to them at the bar, their curiosity was immediately electrified. They felt restless to find out something about these strangers and play that eternal game of picking and choosing. The boy stepped across the flagstone floor on a path he had so often trod and casually placed his hand upon the brass railing where he dwelt and as he waited to be served he ran his finger idly along the condensation on the tap reflecting his morphed image.

It's amazing how much one hears if only you stand close and listen – he heard the one with harsh features and a short black bob say something about the word "greeted", about how it was always misused in the context of those arriving upon scenes of massacre – the other laughing and telling her not to get too hung up on it; but as he stood there listening he visualised all the documentaries he had watched and decided, with a smile, that she was right. She reminded him of someone, he tried to grasp who, but all the comparisons collapsed in a deluge of hybridised rubble – her nose was aquiline yet placed among a phalanx of harsh equipage and large grey eyes. She looked regal to him: this stranger. Thinking the things a nineteen year old thinks about a girl but will only reveal under duress, he offered them drinks, and soon, despite the other girl's reluctance, all four were rumbling through the night in a taxi towards the south side with the streetlamps buzzing past like hornets' tails in a clear sky peppered with silver bite marks.

To live your life is to flick your fingers through a large loose-leafed book; you glimpse some colours, see some and miss many. In a club many colours are missed; blended with neon seeds and grimacing faces one's true future can be lost in an instant. They kissed in all the clumsiness of youth, placing a hand upon a camber unknown several hours previous tasting what each other had drank, immersed in honest attraction. Do we not all hope that another will acknowledge us, draw us near, set us apart among the throng of faces; the destitution leaves time for little else, the peak of one's hope being the possession of a key to a door through which one can pass unchallenged to affection. And then she was gone; as he returned to their seat he saw her leave with another, he saw her face for a final time trying to obtain the words to grant the moment definition – all this pensive apprehension self conscious youth and fears expectant now evidenced in a vision of departure.

It was late now and they became partners in sorrow: the other girl and he, for his friend had long left. Consoling each other as people do: loss being his lot, isolation hers – they joined hands in a society of sadness. And in the morning they spoke.

Its not that she doesn't like you ye know, its just, that was her ex and well, well she's pregnant with his child, so you know they've stuff to sort out

I understand. Well thanks for last night it was great!

Yea it's fine it was fun.

I better be off. Ok.

Well bye then, speak soon.

Bye.

A slow succession of days passed, days furnished with air, light, noise, silence, truce, feigned bliss and black: all the shades of a lonely person's palate, and he thought about her. When a week had gone by one morning passing a faculty notice board he saw a face on a poster in black and white with the words: "mark" and "respect" somewhere in the text – all the lines at once were drawn tightly together and he saw her face, but not in black and white; he had an image in his mind of a vessel within a vessel and rumours he had heard and dismissed. He remembered a hearse pass him two days ago with a wreath spelling sister in crimson and the moment he had passed a bus shelter in which her friend sat head in hands visibly upset. He had been worried, but now he felt that heady mix of relief and guilt at not being the cause of her sadness.

When you go somewhere new you meet people, they see you, for paths intertwine, and the heart is a garden of ever winding paths. I'm one of those people who likes to be alone, to walk and think and look; often I'll walk as far as Bearsden or Linn Park and I'll stand around an uprooted tree, or in one of those large bay windows I'll see a boy and his dog staring out seemingly at nothing, the dog with his paws on the back of the settee, his eyes asking: for what are we looking? All of this passes the time but what I like best is to go to the cinema, the Grosvenor or anywhere really, I sit there in the shadows and when I hear a line like: 'there are few things sadder than a dead bird's wing', I wonder, is that sombre? When a scene elicits grief and when I hear people weep behind and next to me I wonder, is this sad? And I ask myself with what do their tears truly commune. Why do they cry? For tomorrow, for now; perhaps they are crying for someone, perhaps they cry for someone submerged and trapped while others embrace, while others dance.

Same City, Different Maps

Richard Mooney

I am not a resident of Glasgow. I live about an hour away by train. I didn't grow up here in Glasgow; I don't have any fond childhood memories or a Glaswegian accent or an intricate knowledge of the streets and avenues that spread across the map. So instantly I'm at a disadvantage. But before you condemn my work for being in this collection let me explain myself. When I was in the fourth year of my high school career all the budding, bright eyed young students had to be broken to the harsh realities of the workplace. So the school sent us off to find a job for a week. Eventually I was able to grab a last minute place at the Hunterian Museum located in the University of Glasgow. Essentially my position was to shadow the head of the museum and she would assign me to various tasks. Now terrible as it may seem but I had never taken public transport to Glasgow before nor had I been anywhere else in Glasgow other than Buchanan Street, so the prospect of having to travel up to Glasgow, on public transport and find my way to the university was utterly terrifying.

Help was at hand though. And it came in the form of a retired postman. My Uncle John, an enthusiast of the arts was a lover of good music and even better literature. He fuelled my love of literature by introducing me to the classic writers and delivering scores of books ranging from textbooks to sci-fi pulp fiction and we discussed practically everything in-between. When I relayed this situation I found myself in he took it upon himself to help me. He knew the area well as he frequently visited it. So the Saturday before my week as a 'working man' he took me up and showed me exactly how to get to the university. As we made our way up he took a note of what to do, prices, directions, bus numbers, times of arrivals and departures, the lot. When we arrived at the university he showed me the large dark building with its towering spire and went 'That's the university'. Prepared with my extensive instructions I was ready to strike out on my own. On Monday morning, determined to make a good impression I wore a suit, shined my shoes and donned a new tie. Unfortunately due to utter naivety I didn't think about morning traffic. I mean, who will be driving up to Glasgow at half eight in the morning? I was damn near an hour late. So much for my good impression.

My mentor for the week was a young woman with blonde hair tied back firmly. She was polite enough but you could tell she had a lot to get done and my presence was more a hindrance than anything. She ushered me out of her office a moment after meeting her and I was handed over to a colleague of hers. I knew she was just bumping me off for more important things and I accepted it on account of my tardiness but the gentlemen whose care I was now in was very welcoming. My first duty was to learn about where I was, not just the museum, but the whole University. You know that feeling you get when you make a sudden revelation? That's what I got when I was told that the building I thought was *the* university (i.e. the main building that housed the Hunterian Museum) was only *part* of the university. I was awestruck when I looked around at all the different structures; the terraced townhouses that lined University Avenue, the brutalist structure of terrifying proportions that was the library and of course the main building in its full Victorian style looking very Hogwarts-esque. They were all just parts of the picture that made up the whole. All this was learned on a leisurely walk around the campus where the guy explained what each building was, who it was named after and why and what went on in them. I couldn't help it, but I was falling in love with the idea of university, or more specifically the University of Glasgow. When I met back up with my 'employer' she was in a much brighter mood having lightened her workload (I can only assume). My tour guide had vanished and I was left in her company, suddenly we were inspecting exhibits together. I got to know the woman better and realised her first impression on me had been inaccurate as well. She was a warm woman who enjoyed her job and all the challenges it brought. She outlined her plans to revamp the museum, making it bigger and better. Through that little session all my initial fears dispersed and I felt comfortable with her, my morning fiasco behind us. Throughout the week I was rarely by her side though as each morning I would step into her office (on time!) and be issued with a place and a person to answer to. One day I'd be in the art gallery, the next in the Zoology building. The week was a flurry of people and places and was over far too quickly for my liking. On the Friday afternoon I said my final goodbye and departed the university. However a seed had been planted deep inside me and as it grew so would my desire to return to the world I had stepped inside that week. The things I could learn there! The things I could do! The possibilities seemed endless.

Two years later I am sitting in my hall waiting for the post to arrive. It was exam results day. All I needed to see was an 'A' next to a subject, any subject and I would be ready to return to the university having worked for it the past two years. The postman rang the doorbell and I swear if there was an Olympic event for 'running down your hall and opening the door' I would have taken gold for my performance that morning. He handed me over a large white envelope, said 'Good luck' and left. Exam results are stressful enough but the added pressure was making me ill. I then went through the four stages of opening exam results;

Stage 1 - hand the letter to someone else stating that you 'can't do it'.

Stage 2 - snatch the letter back saying something along the lines of 'No! I'll do it, it's my results'.

Stage 3 - break down and refuse to open the envelope for fear of failure.

Stage 4 - Finally open the letter before your family can wrestle it off of you.

A few months later I'm standing at the reception desk of the newly refurbished Hunterian Museum asking if I can speak to my old employer. Moments later a woman with tightly tied back blonde hair sees me from across the room. There is a spark of recognition in her face as she approaches. I notice it and play it cool even though I'm secretly overjoyed that I'm not totally forgettable. The next half hour is spent discussing future exhibitions the museum will hold. Before we part ways she asks me if I'm studying at the university or just up for the open day. I grin, 'I'm studying here. I got my final A in English so I'm coming here to start studying English Literature.'

My only regret is that I never got to formally say thank you to her. I doubt she realised what she had done at the time or even now how she affected my life. But as I sit here, in this brutalist structure of terrifying proportions thinking of what to write for this collection I felt that this would be a fitting place to thank my unsung heroes of that time. My Uncle John to whom I will always be grateful to for helping me decide what I wanted to do in life and to Monica Callaghan, the head of education at the Hunterian museum who exposed me to the university I would fall in love with and later return to study at.

So that's my defense, I am a student of the University of Glasgow and a proud one at that.

December 26th 2010

Mark Fraser

'Aw fuck. Aw FUCK!'

'Shit. Ye hink he's seen us?'

Fae through the holes in his balaclava ah could see Ronnie's eyes dartin aboot. Noo, by an large he generally looks pretty panicked – he's just goat wan ey they faces that always look scared ey somethin – but at this particular conjecture he wis legitimately pantin his shants. Ah wis telt by an associate ey mine who worked in this shoap that their motion sensor burglar alarm was actin up, an he telt me that if we could jimmy the back door open an no break any ey the windaes (cuz the alarm oan the windaes still worked, he says) then aw the gear would be oors fur the takin. However, the cunt failed tae tell me that they'd hired some geriatric ex-copper tae keep an eye oan the shoap, so when ah seen him ah wis ragin. He wis movin slowly between the aisles an he thought he'd try tae reason wae us,

'Right, ah know yer in here ya coupla sods. If ye come oot ah'll no phone the polis an we'll jist call it even.'

But we baith knew he wis full ey shite. He wis swingin his torch aboot the place like a lightsabre, ready tae cut baith us pricks doon the second it touched us. Ah wisnae fur gettin' caught.

'Aw fuck.'

'Mate, fuck this. Ah telt ye this wis a stupid idea. Ah'm sure ye could borrow an amp fae somewan. S'no like theft wis yer only option. Ah'm oota here.'

Ah grabbed him by his troosers as he tried tae staun up; this cunt was gaun naewhere.

'Aye? N go where? The exits' back there behind Darth fat arse. N besides, these cunts kin afford it wi the amount ey money they make. Much ye hink hauf these geetars cost at stock price? Everyhin's inflated tae fuck in these music shoaps an they're insured oot the arse.'

Ronnie poked his heed roond the counter tae eye up the situation an wance he realised it wis as grim as ah hud described, he changed his tune.

'Eh. Shit. Aye. Well...'

Ah could see he was tremblin. So wis ah, but no oota fear ye understand; cuz ey the adrenaline.

'Exactly. Gie's a minute tae hink.'

Ah took a swatch ere the counter tae see the security gaird walking doon the aisle adjacent tae the counter like a fat fuckin fluorescent Santa.

'Here!' a quick whisper from Ronnie demanded ma attention.

'Ah hink we should just head tae the front ey the shoap, tan the windae wi somethin, climb oot it an boot it doon the street. Ye hink?'

'Ah hink that's a shite idea tae be honest mate. We'll set aff the burglar alarm. An besides ah'm no leavin here wi oot somethin. That's a fact, so it is.'

'Aye? Well yer oan yer ain then. Ah'm aff.'

Afore ah could say anyhin Ronnie was makin a beeline fur the front ey the shoap, hoofin it doon the aisle like he wis bein chased by a lion. An sure enough the security gaird clocked um, swung his lightsabre doon oan him, an tried tae mobilize his rotund arse intae a pacey wobble as Ronnie bolted like a startled gazelle. Ah put ma heed ere the counter an ah could see him bombin it in ma direction so naturally ah stuck ma foot oot an as just as he goat clear ey the counter he caught ma shoe an went flyin like lime green Santa Claus, sans reindeer, takin oot a whole row ey geetars. Turned oot it wis the perfect diversion cuz nae amount ey Jedi skills wur gonnae stoap me, ah kin tell ye that fur nothin. Ronnie hud failed tae notice this though an wis promptly wielding an amp at shoulder height, ready tae pan the front windae. So ah shouted ere at him,

'Haw, Ronnie. Mon! The gaird's suddenly found it in himsel tae come roond tae oor way ey thinkin.'

He dropped the amp an looked roond, seen that the gaird wis currently indisposed with a geetar or two wrapped roond his heed an ran ere.

'Nice work Jackie boy! Ye hink the chances ir that he's phont the polis already?'

'Pretty high, Ronnie. Pretty fuckin high indeed.'

'The fuck we gonnae dae? This fuckin hing's gonnae be on CCTV!'

Ronnie sat doon oan the flair. Ah hudnae contemplated it, ah must admit, but he wis right; this whole catalogue ey errors wis gonnae make a pretty fuckin fine entry in tae the Strathclyde Metropolitan Police's very ain incompetent burglars edition of 'You've Been Framed'.

'Ach nane ey yer shite. We've kept oor faces covered n that. We'll be fine.'

'Mate, ah hink ah can hear sirens.'

Ronnie wis trembling again. His adrenaline hud given ower tae pure fear, an it looked like he wis startin tae panic when in reality there wur nae sirens approaching. Yet. But ah felt sure that wis gonnae be rectified in oor immediate future.

'Right. Wir no gonnae get an amp oot ey here the night if that fat cunt's phont the polis. Too heavy an too much hassle. Grab wan ey they PRS geetars an ah'll grab this Les Paul here – geetars are lighter an easier tae transport.'

'Aye, awright. But what aboot an amp? Wir aff oan tour in less than a week.'

'Fuck it man. Ah'll punt these on ebay or sommat. Fuck knows. Ah'll figure it oot. The next time ah walk in here ah'll be a financially solvent individual, free fae the burden ey tour poverty, ready tae make a purchase oan a nice new amp.'

'Here mate, this is bollocks. How could ye no just buy wan yerself an get it oan credit or something?'

'Ye hink ah'm fuckin made ey money? Listen mate; there is nae way in hell ah'm gonna sign ma life away tae a bank through hire purchase or finance or whitever shite it is they dae rip ye aff wi interest these days.'

'Aye, awright Jack, chill oot. It's no exactly like the Provy or Bright Hoose or Wonga.com, like.'

'Naw but it's the principle ey the hing, Ronnie. These fuckin shoaps kin afford to lose some gear noo n then. That's the thing; when the banks are haunin oot bonuses tae cunts that seem tae lose money fur a livin, keepin the workin man doon in the process, then it stauns tae reason that the insurance companies that own them urnae short a few qui– och fuck this, ye know the script mate. Ah'm no staunin here in the back ey a guitar shoap doon the Trongate giein ye a lecture when – '

Something wis up. Ah turned roon tae see wit Ronnie wis lookin at an there wur two polis peerin through the windae. They hudnae seen us yet, thank fuck, cuz there wis a causal nonchalance aboot their movement. Wan ey thum tried the door but tae nae avail. By this point me n Ronnie are oan the deck, prone. Ronnie whispers tae us, 'Mate. We're fucked.'

'Just calm yerself mate. We're no fucked yit. Oan three ah want ye tae jump up, grab a geetar n gie it the Usain Bolt oot the back door, awright? We're gettin oot ey this pal. As punk rock as getting jailed a few days afore a tour is, ah really don't want tae be sent doon for robbery. If we get caught this close tae the Barras they're gonnae hink we're mad junkies lookin to rob some shite. An that'll fuck oor reputation right up tae. Right, ye ready?'

'Aye.'

Naw, he wisnae an neither wis ah, but Ronnie wis in nae position tae argue n frankly, oot of aw the fuckin insane plans ah'd ever hud this wis definitely no wan ey ma favourites. We wur oot ey options; we hud tae get oot ey there pronto.

'Right. Three, two, wan… GO! FUCKIN' GO, RONNIE!'

It wis almost as if ah could see in slow motion: the attitude ey the polis changed fae that ey bobbys just casually dain their roonds, tae that ey a coupla bloodhounds that'd just goat a whiff ey some fresh meat at the realisation that there wir in fact a couple ey chancers in the very shoap they wur scoutin oot. So ah grabbed a geetar n Ronnie done the same an we ran intae the labyrinthine stock room n negotiated the musical equipment like some kind ey jailbird Kypton Factor; if ye fuck this up ye don't just loose yer chance at winnin some shitey trophy, ye'd be loosin yer freedom tae the Sherriff Court, Legal Aid, a shitey free lawyer an aboot six tae eight months in the Bar L. Nae question. Ah booted open the back door n we legged it doon the street. Efter a block, me n Ronnie parted ways. We baith knew where tae meet, ah was just hopin we fuckin goat there.

When ah goat tae the meetin place ah could still feel ma hert poundin in ma ears; ah hink ah musta ran fur aboot hauf a mile tae get the bus back oot tae Darnley. The truth ey the matter is that nickin stuff is a bit ey a mugs game, an ah'm no just sayin that cause ah've changed ma ways or anythin; aw that shite I said tae ye earlier about insurance companies n that is true, it's just that efiter waitin for aboot three hours Ronnie's fat arse never showed up. It later turned oot that the cunt goat nabbed by the polis. The daft prick musta decided tae run back doon the Trongate an it's pretty hard to act inconspicuous as ye run away fae a guitar shoap tae the beat ey a burglar alarm. Ye cannae exactly saunter past two polis wi a geetar ere wan shoulder an the sound of a burglar alarm ere the other an try tae act normal. He said he wis chased fur a few streets up tae that Sally Army hostel in Clyde Street afore launchin the geetar in the Clyde alang wae his balaclava n his jaikit. That wis the first time the polis saw his face; later oan he telt me that they let him go cuz the CCTV footage doesnae huv his face in it. It's probably a load ey shite, but its fair put the frighteners oan me, ah kin tell ye that. Ah'll need tae keep a low profile. Well, efter ah punt this geetar n come back that fae tour, obviously.

Glasgow Story

Sarita Sinkha

As I touched down on Scottish soil, I peered out of the tiny airplane window, spattered in raindrops. 'Green Hollow', I thought to myself, 'that's what Glasgow, means, isn't it?'

As I lugged my 25 kilogram suitcase out of the airport and jumped into a shiny black, beetle-like taxi, the only thing I could think about was how much I missed Moscow. Even though I'm of mixed heritage – half Indian half Russian – I was brought up in Moscow. Moscow was always home for me.

We drove through the city, rain pattering at the windows and the sky covered in a thick blanket of pale grey. Before I left, my mum kept telling me the weather would be awful and depressing, but to be honest, I quite liked the serenity of the rain.

Glasgow seemed so different to Moscow. Everything seemed to move at a slower pace: the people, the cars, the clouds. Everything seemed so calm and laid back – I liked that. What I found most striking about Glasgow were the lush green parks and the beautiful sandstone buildings, gleaming against the grey skies in their majestic colonial beauty.

Unfortunately, I had missed the first three weeks of university and that is what I dreaded the most. Not only did I miss Freshers' Week and knew no one at all, I had to catch up with the work I'd missed, and honestly, medicine is not an easy subject!

I walked to university on my first day, Monday 3rd of October, with my flat-mate Simone – a lovely Portuguese girl and my first friend in Glasgow. As I walked up to the Wolfson Medical School Building, my presence in Glasgow started to feel more real. Before I was reluctant to appreciate the reality of moving alone to a completely foreign country. The impressive contemporary glass facade of the building reflected the magnificent old university building which towered over the West End of Glasgow. Staring at the reflection of the ancient tower in the tinted glass of the medical building, I felt as though I was leaving my previous life behind and starting a new journey.

As clichéd as it may sound, I was afraid that I would not be able to understand the Scottish accent, but surprisingly, I had no difficulty whatsoever! On the contrary, people found it difficult to understand me. 'So where are you from?' I would be asked. 'Russia,' I'd reply, 'I'm half Indian half Russian.' At that point, my somewhat strong American accent would baffle people.

Having spent nearly four months in Glasgow I have learnt to love this beautiful city as much as I loved home. The friendly people, who to me seemed like aliens, as in Moscow, most of the people I saw on the streets usually frowned at you and would never apologize if they accidentally pushed you over, let alone bumped into you; the versatile cultural mix, which gives rise to the most interesting nights out I have ever experienced; the unpredictable weather, which one second will make you want to cry when you get caught in a heavy shower without an umbrella, but the next minute, put a smile on your face as the ominous grey clouds vanish and a luscious rainbow splits the sky into two, brilliant blue halves.

Whenever I come back home and I tell people I study in Scotland, their reply is: 'England?' This now truly makes me angry and I take my time to explain the difference to them. Have I become a true Glaswegian? Maybe.

P.O.B.

James Carson

Fun and games tonight. Just turning into Woodlands Road when I hit black ice. It's no' a taxi I need, it's a pack of fucking huskies. Nae bother for steady Eddie, but. Regained control in a split second.

Quick glance at the back, to make sure he's no' freaking out.

'Fun and games tonight, son!'

Not a flicker. Face stuck in his mobile.

I'd seen him at the bus stop.

'Nae buses on tonight, son.'

So, he jumps in and just says, 'Bennetts.' No 'please', no nothing. Scrawny, looks Indian. And just wearing skinny jeans and a skimpy jerkin.

'No' cold, mate?'

Nothing. I get on the radio to Frank:

'P.O.B. Pickup at Woodlands Road for Glassford Street.'

P.O.B.: that's taxi-speak for prick on board.

Frank says he thinks it's getting better. Is it fuck! Delivery lorry jack-knifed at Sainsbury's, cars and vans skidding about like Wacky Races. Half an hour for a ten minute journey. Know what Heather would have said. But I prefer to be out and about instead of rattling round that shithole on my own.

So, we finally get there and, just as I thought, Bennetts is all locked up. Soon as the snow set in at lunchtime, I knew the city would start shutting down. Didnae tell him, of course. If he wants to waste his money stoating about the winter wonderland it's his lookout.

So I'm waiting for him to pay. Doors locked, and I've got the baseball bat at the ready in case he gets ideas about doing a runner. I've had that wi' Asians before. Only, he just sits there looking out at the club. Snow piling up at the door. They've had it done up, and there's panels with drawings of guys in the buff. Supposed to look like Greek athletes, but it's basically gay porn. Usually jumping on a Friday, and the poofs are good for business. But this isnae a night for the stilettos.

'Listen, son, if you want back to Woodlands Road I'll have to put the meter back on.'

And that's when he starts crying.

And we're no' talking a sniffle. This is like Niagara. Bloody hysterics. Cannae understand a word, I'm shouting through the glass.

'Look, son, calm down, will you? What's the matter?'

Bawling his heid off, no idea what he's on about. Then, I notice the cafe opposite is still open.

'Listen, son, how about a coffee?'

I can tell Frank's no' happy at me taking a break, what with the buses off, but fuck him. Brian and Danny and the rest of them are sitting on their arses watching Ice Road Truckers while I'm out in the real thing.

Lassie behind the counter's glued to the telly and I have to rap on the table to get her face away fae bloody Desperate Housewives.

'Didnae think you'd be open tonight.'

She shrugs, mumbles something about living just round the corner. Needs the money, Christmas coming up. Looks like she's about to start bubbling. And I think, bloody hell, no' another one. I get a couple of black coffees and scoop up a handful of milks and sugars.

He's staring out the window, face still tripping him. But the floodgates have closed, thank Christ, and there's even a wee smile when I set his coffee down. I'm just planning to add the drinks to his fare when he pipes up, 'That's where I met him.'

And I think, here we go.

Says he latched on to this gorgeous guy fae Cumbernauld. I know, that's exactly what I thought. Love at first sight, blah, blah, so he gave the guy his number. Only that was two weeks ago, and – surprise, surprise – he's no' heard back. So, he's been going back to the club every night since then, hoping Romeo will return and sweep him off his feet. Cumbernauld? Dream on.

And he's going on and on about this guy, his curly hair, his perfect wee nose. Enough to give you the boak. Anyway, I just let him ramble on. I start thinking about my breakfast. Might have a fry up when my shift's over. Mibbe even a hot chocolate, because I'm worth it. Snow outside falling on last night's ice. Mair broken legs in the morning.

Next thing I know, he's looking at me, waiting for an answer. Course, I havenae a scooby what he's just said, so I'm sitting there like a fanny. Can see the headlines:

'GLASGOW TAXI DRIVER LOST FOR WORDS. NICOLA STURGEON PROMISES ACTION.'

And he's just about to start the waterworks again when I remember something on breakfast telly this morning. So, I start spouting all this crap:

'Listen, son, the pain never goes away, but you learn to live with it. You've got to achieve closure.'

Load of shite, but he's lapping it up, nodding and smiling. Never thought I'd see the day when Lorraine bloody Kelly would be good for something. So I just carry on:

'Time is a great healer. You've got to build a bridge and get over it.' Utter garbage. Then I hear myself saying, 'Que sera sera', and I'm hoping to Christ he's never heard of...

'Doris Day! I love her movies!' His eyes are lighting up like the Blackpool illuminations. 'I watched Pillow Talk last Sunday afternoon with a box of Quality Street. She's so cool!'

He's smiling now. It changes his whole face. Makes him look like that young lad in Slumdog Millionaire. His name's Vikram. 'Call me Vik.' Says he's seventeen, looks about twelve. I ask if his parents willnae be worried about him.

'My mum's visiting my gran.'

'In India?'

'Bradford.'

'Ah, ok. Your dad?'

'He's working.'

'In India?'

'Iceland.'

'Oh, right. My brother does deliveries for them. Maybe your dad knows...

'Not that Iceland.'

Turns out his father's some high powered something-ologist, studying volcanoes like the one that scuppered our trip to Gran Canaria last year. His family came up fae Yorkshire when Vik got a place at Strathclyde. He's studying architecture. Nearly wets himself going on about how fantastic Glasgow buildings are. He cannae have seen that Cineworld monstrosity.

He asks if I'm married, and I tell him about Heather. Says he's sorry, and was it cancer? He obviously disnae read the papers.

I knew I'd get off. As I said to my brief, you just need to keep it simple: she lost her balance and fell down the stairs. The number of times I've watched courtroom dramas, and the numpty in the dock ties himself up in knots wi' complicated alibis and far-fetched stories. Not steady Eddie. She lost her balance and fell down the stairs.

And now Vik's reaching out and touching my hand, 'I'm so sorry about your wife, Eddie.'

When I look up, his big, brown eyes are on me. I stand up too quickly, bump my knee against the tabletop, clattering the cups.

'I need the loo.'

I blame that fucking volcano. If only we'd got to Spain, it would have been fine. Instead, it was two weeks at home wi' Heather and her own personal rain cloud. Only a matter of time before we blew up at each other, and when we did, my God, it was worse than the bloody volcano.

Grabbed my keys and took off. Still not sure how I ended up at Kelvingrove, but it was great to be away from her crabbit face. Folk out wi' their dogs, mad joggers, lassies sunbathing. Nice.

Must have fell asleep on the grass, 'cause when I woke up it was getting dark. Naeb'dy aboot, so I nipped into the bushes for a pee. That's how it started.

When I get back from the loo, Vik hands me a twenty.

'Thanks for everything, Eddie. You're a really good listener, and so full of good advice.'

I look at him to see if he's taking the piss, but he's actually on the level. Says Scottish folk are so friendly. Aye, son, try taking a night bus tae Cumbernauld and see how friendly they are.

He says he's gonnae walk back. I tell him no' to be daft, I'll take him back, hauf fare. But he'll no' be told. As he puts on his jacket, his shirt rides up and I get an eyeful of his belly. Chocolate-dark.

Became a habit, I suppose. Saturday afternoons were best, just after sunset. Got to know the signals – keys rattling, a cough. Then into the undergrowth. Ugly as fuck, most of them, but if I shut my eyes it was better than nothing. Which is what I'd been getting from Heather. Last time I'd got moist between the sheets wi' her was when her hot water bottle burst. But after a while, you start wanting more than a quickie in the bushes.

'Listen, Vik, give me your number'.

And I can see he's no sure.

'Just to make certain you get home safe. Call me an old softy, but we all need to be there for each other.' (Thanks again, Lorraine.)

He smiles and bends down to jot his number on a napkin. Jet black hair.

She wouldnae let it go. Kept niggling and nipping, wanting to know what was so special about Saturday afternoons. Told her it was none of her business, and surely to God she could go to the bloody wedding herself. Headed for the loo, but she was right up the stairs at my back.

And she's screaming, 'You think I don't know what your game is? You're pathetic, Eddie, you're just a pathetic little man!'

Which is when I slapped her. Which is when she lost her balance and fell down the stairs.

I'll give it a few days. Ring him up, dead casual:

Hi Vik, made some calls, think I've found that guy you're looking for… Aye, sure, I'll take you there myself…

Can pick him up at the same bus stop, stick a coffee in his hand: one of steady Eddie's special blends. By the time he's out for the count we'll be at the park. Big freeze set to last another week, so it'll be dead quiet.

Then it's just me and him.

Unraveled

Louis Pilard

The curtains are torn
Beginning the scene.
Worn ragged, the sky
Cries tears in the morn'
with no fear or scorn.
No voice to reply:
As if you are clean
and clear and reborn.

Now you can walk in Kelvingrove Park
Graveled muddy feet dragged a travelling
silhouette that delved and dove in the dark
Unraveled in the slushy streets
Like used condoms and mushy fags
Lungs crackling and wheezing like crinkled
Plastic shopping bags dancing in the gust of wind
Isn't it beautiful? No it's disgusting.

I don't remember the last time I saw my own shadow
A shadow so invisible and silent

If you do not speak though, sing at least
In whispers like wind in trees
You can hear in the
Song of sighs and drab raps of slighted madness,
Mogwai and Arab Strap and The Twilight Sad
As if they had carefully plucked the rhythms
From soggy leaves and crisp packets spinning
In the breeze.

Spitting a gritty rough cough
I' the Reuch Heuch Hauch
Grey masks glide through shoe shops
Like the souls o' the damned are they
Hungry homeless, 2 for 1 meal deals
Weight watchers, I am not
An alcoholic, I am not
A drug addict, I pod, I pad,
I phone, I am a human being
Just ignore him
Just do it,
Impossible is nothing
Spare change please?
The best a man can get
Looking for company?
Maybe she's born with it.
Life's complicated enough.
Things can only get better
Summer sale, fucking joke
fake tanning, family planning.
Please help me, dear Guardian! Dear
Independent Observer! Please help me,
O Sun! My Daily Star, what's the Big Issue?

Gypsies outside newsagents
Corner shops, refugee camps
Steal our jobs, Chinese Buffet King, Mother India
Take-Aways take me away, Hostages
Closing borders, terrorists and smugglers
Last orders, they dress like gangsters
Hanging out in big groups like that
State shoots civilian protesters
I want to get out of this shitehole
If I go back, they will kill me.
Time for a holiday, Sun causes cancer

Jesus is the answer, Israel, Palestine
Ottomans, Rome, Tibet, Bagdad
From the first libraries in time
My dad came back in a bag.
Migraines, my braces hurt
Lost limbs, hidden mines
Protein shakes, lose weight
African horn starves, drought hits millions
The usual.
Can I just stop you for a minute there?
I'm busy, broke, late, no, just no,
No! Please, please,
Help the blind, help the deaf, help the mute,
Find your eyes, find your sound, find your voice,
Think of the children, Save the children, Oxfam,
Barnardos, SPCC, UNICEFucking brats,
Never stop crying in supermarkets.

He's just back fae Afghanistan
He's ma sexy soldier with a sexy tan
We're all going out the night to get pished
Coz ma sexy soldier dodged the bullets.
Just dance, gonna be okay, dada doodoo mmm
Look at the tits on her. I'm getting a shag
The night, ahm tellin ya. Have you ever
Come on their face like online?
Aye it's class. C'mon have another
Drink. D'you think you're cool?
Aye, smoking is cool. It's like
The birth of the cool.
Smoking damages the health
Of those around you. That's the death
of the cool. He's always flirting
with that bitch over there, ah swear
I'm gonna slap her. Partying partying yeah.

Orite doll, me and you could
Have a bad romance. I've dodged
The bullets. Boom boom boom boom
I want you in my room. Just dance
Dadadadadadadada, doodoodoodoommmmm
Why do they dress like sluts if they don't
Want a shag? They look like pornstars
By about twelve years old. They turn us on
Then make us feel bad for it.
They all think I'm a slut
Take it easy, nice'n'sleazy.
I've got that poster on my wall
Just popped a pill
That says choose life
from Trainspotting, I'm coming up
C'mon just have another drink.
Where are my keys? I've lost my phone.
Got any swedge mate? I'm slipping off
The edge mate. Blinded by the lights
Oh dear, here we go, Dear God 2.0,
Stop telling me to relax
You never give me your money.
The walk home is horrible.
I didn't pull, feeling empty, sick,
Everything looks mingin, like-
Doesn't even feel real now I'm back.
Can hardly tell the difference between
Art galleries and graffiti on the wall,
Berlin and Gaza, can't hear the difference
Between Techno and Wagner.
Common everybody
I don't know how I fucking caught it
Warts are a common occurrence
Among the sexually active - don't be like that

Geez a Glasgae smile, a glasgae kiss
Please, the truth is
I'm scared, of being alone
That's why I try to shag birds, I don't even like doing it
I'm shite at it, I come too quickly and most of them
Don't even stay the night, I've been around but
I love you so much, please, love me
I'm just an idiot sayin' crap, please,
despite my idiosyncrasies.

We sift through the veins of glowing grey
Blocks and breathe malty roars into fog
Jumping circles to smashing bottles
Glitter the roads with our streams of gold
Rivers that flow like blood of the old
Who chase us from their conquered gardens

Our conscious conscience hardens.
Fuck love it's a withered discourse
Made of battered windows and stripped doors
Stolen saliva, sore throats that spit hoarse
Words at pissed whores smelling like sulphates.
Ticking away the moments
That make up a dull day
The blooming heart shivering
Shrivelling down
Into a quivering stone.
Hell isn't other people, it's alone
Watching Friends on the couch
Another sequel or repeat
A life lived in episodes and scenes
A masterful brain switched off
and left to masturbate.
Close the curtains it's getting late.
Hang your universe on a string.

Let the world sing itself to sleep
I will sit back and observe
There is time to kill today
We are all wasted and watching
We are waiting
To discover the different ways
In which we do the same thing.

Anthropology – Music 1920s

Christine Cosh

Music to my Ears… A street musician plays a Strauss Waltz on the violin… The Blue Danube…

This story is based in the West End of Glasgow in the 1920s. Robert and Helen meet in Byres Road and a chance meeting leads to an unhappy outcome in their young lives. The circumstances of their brief affair changes both their worlds and future happiness leaving behind an unspoken promise of never to leave each other. Formal adoption was not introduced in Great Britain until 1928, and most adoptive parents went through ecclesiastical connections or agreements between family and friends. The story unfolds…

The year is April 1921. A young servant girl Helen Spence crosses the road at Byres Road in Glasgow to make her way to the underground, taking her to the south side of Glasgow, known as Plantation, to deliver a note from her employer to a specialist Doctor on Paisley Road West. It is here at the age of fifteen that Helen bumps into Robert McLennan, who is seventeen and a scholar at Glasgow Academy, who is also catching the tube. They both laugh as they scramble down the stairs, just as the doors close and they are suddenly on their own as the train pulls out and the platform falls into complete silence. The young couple look at each other and in that moment their fate is sealed.

Robert is a student at Glasgow Academy and is often in the area, but today, for a special reason, he is visiting the University of Glasgow, encouraged by his headmaster and his Father, a doctor, on the south side of the city. Helen explains to Robert the reason for her trip, and Robert, delighted, offers to escort her for the rest of the afternoon, as it's Helen's afternoon off after the delivery. From opposite ends of the social echelon, the couple are doomed, but at this youthful age they are full of happiness and exuberance: unable to determine or realise that their meeting will result in a great deal of suffering and will haunt them both for the rest of their lives.

With trembling eyes, Helen gazes at Robert and he gazes back, at that moment falling in love unaware of their surroundings; totally absorbed in their happiness. They board the tube and travel to Cessnock together, chatting as if they have known each other for most of their lives. Helen explains her position and Robert his and the reason for his trip to the north side of the city to visit the Department of English Literature, in which he hopes to study. Helen is impressed and embarrassed but Robert puts her at her ease, telling her she is surely the prettiest girl north and south of the city. Helen forgets about her status immediately and is delighted to be in the company of such a charming young man and escort, and with her ladylike qualities manages to fit the requirement by chatting away about subjects she has heard her employers discuss, she is a success, and Robert is truly enchanted.

After the delivery to the specialist, Helen meets Robert at the corner of Paisley Road West. Robert points out where his father's surgery is and suggests that they catch the train to Bellahouston Park, have tea and spend the afternoon in the park. Helen is delighted. This is to be the first of many trips to Bellahouston and the Botanic Gardens, where for the next six months they meet, have tea and walk through the park. It is May 1921, and the young couple seem lost in the business of the city, delighting at their transparency and getting closer each week on Helen's afternoon off.

Her duties at Havelock Street keep her busy and as the weeks pass to months, Helen and Robert are aware of their feelings and the serious direction their relationship is taking. Their kisses grow stronger and their longing to share each other's intimacy is almost unbearable. Until the late afternoon of October when once again they have had afternoon tea, Helen wearing her best shoes and hat and Robert who has managed to miss school once again for the last two months, as during the summer holidays no one suspected, but it is now becoming an issue at school and Robert has to suggest they meet later, after school which gives them both less time together.

Helen cries and they both realise the extent of their feelings for each other and that neither of them are free; this sudden realisation overwhelms them and they consummate their relationship without further hesitation in a quiet dusky evening in the shelter of the Glass House in the Botanic Gardens. Flustered at what has happened, they both run out of the Glass House as it's about to close. Realising they have sealed their love and their fate for the rest of their lives.

As the months pass, the young couple continue to meet in the late afternoons every Wednesday which gives them little privacy, as the realisation that they may never be together as Robert's mother has become suspicious of late night Wednesday expeditions after school. She turns up at school to find him not there; nor has he been for the last three months and of course, she recalls his summer excursions on a Wednesday afternoon. Putting these together, she confronts Robert on his return. He has no choice but to confess to meeting Helen. His parents are outraged and contact Havelock Street where Helen resides and works as a servant, to warn Helen that the meeting is unsuitable.

When Helen is confronted she has no choice but to blurt out she is expecting a baby in the summer of 1922. They are all left speechless and Helen is given the choice of giving the child up for adoption after the birth. Robert is forbidden to see Helen, and he is sent to Melbourne in Australia to finish his studies with his uncle, who has gone into a property business in the city. Immediately, Robert's career and future have been determined by his parents decision and the agreement has been reached that when the baby is born, it will be put up for adoption, Helen refuses to comment on this. However, as the months pass and the misery of facing life without the support and tender love of Robert, Helen's resolve begins to break down. She is bereft at not seeing Robert and as the baby swells her heart breaks. Letters sent to his father's surgery are never passed on. This pushes Helen to despair. She waits every Wednesday at 4.30 pm, hoping he will arrive and confirm their love for each other; he never does. Her son is delivered at Stevenson Drive in Shawlands, at the home of her employer's sister; a little boy. After the birth Helen takes the baby to the father's surgery, where she is threatened and told not to return that Robert now has a new life in Australia and will not be returning in the near future. She resolves to return to her employer at Havelock Street, who suggests that the Captain who lives upstairs, knows of a colleague, a trainee steamer pilot, who is from good stock, honest, hard working and willing to take young Robert for his childless wife, Jessica. The Gillies's are a Christian family with a comfortable home.

After Robert's baptism in Mallig Street, Partick, Helen hands over young Robert named after his father. With her heart breaking she becomes unwell and returns to the island of Rothesay, the place she left to find work in Glasgow. By now Helen is only sixteen but within herself feels more like thirty years.

After many years, Helen marries and has another son, but the heartache she felt over losing Robert and her baby left her bitter and unhappy, with so many dreams unfulfilled. She never told anyone about Robert and her son until she was in her eighty fifth year and spending her last days in an nursing home on the Isle of Bute; when one morning the assistant carer a young women called Roberta called in to see her. Helen liked Roberta; not only because of her name, but because her bright happy personality reminded her a little of herself some seventy years before. Helen was crying so badly when Roberta tried to comfort her, it was to no avail. Helen uncontrollably explained how she had to give up her baby seventy years ago and how every day she weeps alone but today she wanted to tell someone before she died.

Helen said, 'ultimately in life you are on your own, but I have felt this acutely since the day I gave up my beautiful baby boy Robert. But in the 1920s, girls who were servants had little choice. The only comfort I have is that the childless woman adored Robert, and this was a great comfort to me over the years. Now that I have shared my secret, I can die in peace. There were so many girls like me between the First and Second World Wars, who were never given a choice. Perhaps I will meet Robert in heaven and hold him once more in my arms.'

Helen closed her eyes, and Roberta thought this was from exhaustion but she had passed on peacefully after sharing the burden she had hidden for seventy years, she would at last see her great love and their son in heaven, she believed she would meet them again. Somewhere in the distance there is a light waltz being softly played.

When Helen's son Bill arrived at the home after news of his mother's death, he mentioned to the Care Manager that Helen had mentioned to him on his previous visit how happy she was because of the company of a young woman called Roberta. Bill said, 'She seemed so excited and happy to talk about this young career'.

The matron looked astonished but went on to say, 'we don't have a carer of that name.'

Bill hesitated and said, 'Yes, I am sure that is what she said!'

The matron nodded. 'Just before an elderly person dies, we often hear stories of carers we don't have, it must be one of the angels.

They both sighed and smiled, whether they believed it or not.

As Bill turned to leave, the matron said, 'we never get to know our parents in our life time. Sometimes it is within these walls that truths and lies are revealed, just before we say goodbye and depart for our next.'

Toast to Strathclyde's Bravest

Liam Patrick Hainey

On a toilet wall,
In the South Side:

"Jim the fireman
from just down the road
is a wank,
With no morals,
or honour."

To Jimmy!

Biographies

Deborah Andrews is currently working towards a PhD in Creative Writing (AHRC funded) at Glasgow University. Previously, she's worked as a theatre director/writer, co-founding Solar Bear in 2002 (where she was Artistic Director 2002-2009). Her short stories have been published in several anthologies, and she is now completing her first novel.

Dr Laura Bissell lectures in Theatre Studies at the University of Glasgow and teaches on the Contemporary Performance Practice BA Honours course at the Royal Conservatoire of Scotland (formerly the RSAMD). Laura's research explores feminism, technology and performance and her interests include writing poetry and writing for performance.

Karen Bradley is a keen cartoon illustrator using both traditional ink and contemporary digital techniques. Her recent Glasgow School of Art evening class 'Comic Books and Graphic Novels' has inspired her to venture into the comic world. Karen studied English at Strathclyde University and currently works at BBC Scotland.

Stephanie Brown quit her job last year to start the MLitt Creative Writing course and become a freelance writer. She has never looked back since.

Alice Bugg: Born a long time ago in Wales, not dead yet, though various bits don't work so well. Proudest achievement: three sprogs, all tall, good-looking and exceptionally nice. Writes. Sometimes. Makes a mean lasagne.

Dr Robin Burgess: I have lived and worked in Glasgow for the past 3 years, having moved from Nottingham where I studied for my PhD in Biosciences. My current post is as Research Information Manager at The Glasgow School of Art. I have a real love of the arts and music, and enjoy bringing my creative side into the predominantly data driven work that I do. I like to write little ditties and draw and the city of Glasgow has been inspirational for helping me to pursue my outside interests in the creative arts.

Graham Campbell: I am a Jamaican London Scots poet specialising in the interplay of the 3 languages I use. I am African & Caribbean Network – Secretary which means I am the founder and manager of the African Caribbean Centre which I established through the A&CN in 2009. *I'm no a zombie* is about my experiences in being greeted in Glasgow, even more so now that a Scots filmmaker Kevin McDonald has made that film about Bob Marley!

James Carson is from Glasgow. His stories, articles and reviews have been published in magazines and anthologies, in print and online. James is currently studying Creative Writing in Glasgow University's celebrated MLitt programme.

John Conlon: I am 32 years of age, originally from Newbridge, Ireland. I studied English Literature at the University of Maynooth, and have been living in Scotland for six years; during this time I have worked for Waterstones in Edinburgh and recently embarked upon an MSc in Information Management and Preservation at Glasgow University.

Jose Manuel Correa Rollano: Novelist and short-story writer. Was born on January 1st, 1989 in Medellín, Colombia. Studied primary and high school in Colombia. In 2007 moved to Montreal (Canada) and studied French for a year. In 2008 started Marketing and International Logistics at The Sabana University in Bogota (Colombia). In 2009 started Business and Management at the University of Glasgow and is currently studying there.

Christine Cosh: Born in Bellahouston, Glasgow, arrived at Glasgow University at a mature student after achieving a Diploma in Acting and Performance This was a platform to continue study in chosen subjects Music and History. Earlier career consisted of 30 years in business and management in the heart of Glasgow.

George Craig's stories have been published in *FromGlasgowtoSaturn*, placed runner-up in the Guardian Short Story Competition and shortlisted for the Bridport Prize. He completed the Faber Academy's Novel Writing course (2010), graduated with distinction from Glasgow University's MLitt (2011) and is currently working on a novel and a collection of stories.

Paul Deaton's poetry has been long-listed for the Bridport Prize and published in *The Spectator*. In 2010 he was runner-up in the Arvon International Poetry Competition. Bristol based, his ancestors are Scottish, Gordons and MacDonalds – for some reason this feels important and led him to study at GU.

Samuel Devereux: Currently living in Glasgow after being led across the border by the rains, enrolled at Glasgow School of Art, spending most of his time staring out of windows, making videos and practicing his handwriting.

Ruth Dunster is currently working on a PhD at the University of Glasgow, on Autism, Theology and the Arts. She first began writing in *Survivors Poetry Scotland* in the 1990s, and her poetry and short stories have been published in a variety of anthologies and publications. She lives near Glasgow.

Mark Fraser is a 26 year old Scottish Literature student/man-child who has been writing since as far back as he can remember. He is a punk rock fanatic and currently runs a music website. This is the first piece of prose he has had published and he's chuffed to bits.

Frankie Gault: When I stopped taking alcohol 6 years ago, it was for any number of valid reasons. Mainly, though, I wanted to preserve my sanity, and after a sweaty, nervous year, I decided to try writing. I wanted to know who I was, who I am and who I might become. My very patient wife Helen played a starring role in this and I was ably supported by a stellar cast consisting of my friends, tutors and classmates from the University and the Centre for Open Studies

David Gourlay was born in Glasgow in 1960 He has worked for over 30 years in the School of Engineering David is married with two children and is currently putting the finishing touches to his first novel.

Liam Patrick Hainey was born in Glasgow and his lived there for most of his life (spending the rest of it in the town of Falkirk). He is currently a student at Glasgow University studying Scottish Literature. In his spare time he enjoys cricket, football and music.

Brian Hamill grew up in Airdrie but has lived in Partick since 2009. He has a BA in English Literature from the University of Strathclyde and an MSc in I.T. from the University of Glasgow. He has attended creative writing classes at the University of Glasgow DACE since 2008.

Helen Kellock: I am an English Literature student from Glasgow. Before beginning my literature studies my background was in the visual arts and continues to be a practice of mine. As a result I have developed an interest in interdisciplinary work, namely in the interaction between word and image.

Andrew Latimer is a student of English literature and a writer of occasional light verse.

Sarah-Ann Lee: 22, Female, Odd. Sometimes goes by 'Schwa', with an often schwaverage life. Not really a silent vowel though.

Aonghas Mac Leòid was brought up in Inverness, moving to Edinburgh as a 15 year old. A fluent Gaelic speaker, he often stays with family on the Isle of Barra. He has lived in Glasgow for six years and is working towards a PhD in Celtic, looking at 20th Century long poems.

Calum MacLeòid writes and translates poetry and short stories in Gàidhlig, Invernessian and English. He has recently begun researching his dissertation which will be on the novels of Tormod Caimbeul. Probably.

Micaela Maftei is originally from Toronto. She moved to Scotland in 2007 and studied at the University of Glasgow.

James Malcolm is a Glasgow-based writer and film editor. He's studying for an MLitt in Creative Writing at the University of Glasgo, and is working on a screenplay for his final portfolio.

My name is **Maria-Ioana Marchidanu,** I am twenty, and I come from Romania. I am a first – year student at the University of Glasgow, studying Literature and Art History. For me, creative writing has always been like an old and dear friend, inspiring me to be a better person

Imogen Marcus was born in London in 1985. She graduated from St Johns College, Oxford and has lived in Glasgow since 2007. She is currently a postgraduate student of English Language at the University of Glasgow, completing her PhD thesis on the language of Bess of Hardwick's sixteenth century letters.

James Leo McAskill was born in Manchester in 1989. He enjoys the sea but not swimming. He is primarily a poet and currently resides in Glasgow. He can be reached at james.l.mcaskill@hotmail.co.uk.

Ellen McAteer works at the Glasgow School of Art, and is a graduate of the University of Glasgow. A member of the Clydebuilt Verse Apprenticeship Scheme, she has been published in magazines and anthologies, had a play at the Edinburgh Fringe recorded for radio, and won a BBC songwriting competition.

Richie McCaffery (b. 1986) is a Carnegie scholar at the University of Glasgow, researching for a PhD on the Scottish poetry of World War Two. He has recently enjoyed a Hawthornden fellowship and in August will take up a Brownsbank writer's retreat. His first pamphlet collection *Spinning Plates*, from HappenStance, was published in March 2012.

Mairi McCloud: I am an American student studying archaeology and Scottish Gaelic. I was raised with a strong sense of Scottish heritage and identity and when I decided to go to university (after spending several years working and traveling), Glasgow was the perfect choice, as it feeds my several passions for archaeology, family history, Gaelic and classic films.

Scott McGowan grew up in Milton of Campsie, a small village northeast of Glasgow. He graduated in Sculpture at Glasgow and Winchester Schools of Art and is a practising artist. Recently he has been translating some of these experiences into writing. He now lives in Innellan, near Dunoon.

Shauna McMullan is an artist and part time lecturer in the Department of Sculpture and Environmental Art at Glasgow School of Art. "Something about a word" was developed as a public artwork for Eastgate, Bridgeton. Design and computer work by Paul Hughes.

Richard Mooney is a student at Glasgow University doing English Literature and born in the small town of Greenock. His first piece of writing was published in an anthology of creative writing called *Tip Tap Flat*. A foundation he wishes to build upon in the near future.

Emeline Morin was supposed to study in Scotland for a year only, but fell in love with Glasgow. She is now doing a PhD at Glasgow University, working mostly on dark fairy-tales retellings. She hopes to become both a scholar and a writer. Find out more at: http://emelinemimiemorin.wordpress.com/.

Eleanor Morton is a second year student from Edinburgh, studying English Literature. She was previously at St. Andrews University, but transferred to Glasgow to complete her degree. She enjoys writing and performs stand-up comedy. Her favourite authors include M.R. James, W. M. Thackeray, and other people with too many initials.

Jordan Mulligan was born in 1991. Originally from Falkirk, Jordan now lives and studies in Glasgow. He is a student of English Literature at Glasgow University. He is an aspiring poet, living off low wages and cuppa soup and is slowly learning to like cats.

Theresa Muñoz was born in Vancouver, Canada and now resides in Edinburgh. She is an Overseas Research Scholar writing her doctoral dissertation on the work of Tom Leonard. She published poems in *Canadian Literature*, *New Writing Scotland*, *The Frogmore Papers* and many others. Her pamphlet *Close* is available from HappenStance Press.

Julie Pallesen: I was born in Copenhagen in 1988. After finishing high school in Denmark, I moved to Glasgow to study sculpture at the art school. I write all kinds of things from letters to lists, but perhaps mainly I like to write short prose

Louis Pilard: a self-proclaimed Scot of French nationality and descent. He enjoys thinking, drinking, walking, boxing, eating, sexing, talking, laughing, walking, helping, yelping, writing, marinating, lazing, waiting, wasting and many other activities. Often paranoid and confused until stumbling upon rare moments of clarity andtfulfilment A fan of irritating noises.

Jamie Pilc: When I was thirteen some Russians liked my story about a snail who lived in IKEA. From then on I've written bits of fiction, some of them getting quite big and out of hand and often involving pirates. I'm finishing third year of University just now, it's been nice.

Julie Ramage: Julie is GSA's Senior Research Manager and founder of the Facebook art sit, Domestic Art Movement. English by birth, Julie has lived in Scotland since 1994 and has two children. Julie's contribution to this volume, Maggot, was a fluke. She just wrote down something she overheard at Buchanan Bus Station.

Alastair Reid: I am currently in my third year of architectural study at the Mackintosh School of Architecture and was encouraged to write a piece of poetry as part of a studio project. Since then I have written several in the Scots language. The featured poem was read at the MSA Burns Supper.

Alan Riach (b.1957), Professor of Scottish Literature at Glasgow University, General Editor of the *Collected Works of Hugh MacDiarmid*, President of the Association for Scottish Literary Studies (2006-2010), author of *Representing Scotland in Literature, Popular Culture and Iconography* (2005) and, with Alexander Moffat, *Arts of Resistance: Poets, Portraits and Landscapes of Modern Scotland* (2008), described by the *Times Literary Supplement* as 'a landmark book'. His poems are collected in *This Folding Map* (1990), *An Open Return* (1991), *First & Last Songs* (1995), *Clearances* (2001) and *Homecoming* (2009).

H.J. Rodgers is currently a student on the University of Glasgow's MLitt in Creative Writing. Born in Yorkshire, she has previously had her work published by *Route* and performed by The White Rabbit Theatre Company. In April 2012, Hannah was announced as the joint winner of the Martin Wills Award for Writing.

Mohamed Rokadiya: I am a final-year undergraduate studying English Literature with French. During my time in Glasgow, I have been fortunate enough to study courses ranging from French philosophy to Postcolonialism. As for poetry, the tutelage and direction warmly offered by both Kei Miller and Michael Schmidt have been wholly invaluable.

Stewart Sanderson is twenty one and was born in Glasgow, where he is currently working towards an MPhil by research in Scottish Literature. His poems have appeared in various journals, including *Magma*, *Gutter* and *The Literateur*. He regularly contributes translations and original poetry to *Lallans* magazine.

Suzanne Scott has been writing poetry since the mid-1980's and has collected over 2000 poems: theprophetess.co.uk. Suzanne has been published in many magazines including *Orbis*, *Moonstone*, and *Fire*; she was recently invited to the South Bank Centre in London to read her poetry at the Fire farewell event. After an MA in English at St Andrews, she did a PhD in English at Glasgow University. She currently works in Particle Physics at Glasgow.

Sophie Sexon studies English Literature at the University of Glasgow. Sophie moved to London at the age of sixteen to train as an actress before returning home to pursue her career in academia. She now enjoys playing flute and singing in a number of bands around Glasgow.

My name is **Sarita Sinkha** and I am a first year medical student. I am of mixed Russian/Indian heritage and have lived all my life in Moscow. After moving to Glasgow I have experienced a completely different culture, which has inspired me to write my short story.

Siobhan Staples was born in England but moved to the Scottish Borders at the age of six. Having flitted back and forth ever since, she finds the question 'where are you from?' impossible to answer. Siobhan is studying Creative Writing at Glasgow Uni and is co-editor of *From Glasgow to Saturn*.

Amanda Stewart currently works in the Fine Art Office of the Glasgow School of Art. She has a Degree in Graphic Design & Multimedia from Glasgow Caledonian University and has recently rediscovered her interest in Graphic Storytelling, Sequential Art and Comics.

Ellie Stewart writes poetry where she can; mostly on the train between Bathgate and Glasgow. She is a winner of the John Muir Trust poetry competition and one of the editors of Ironstone. Other poems can be read online in *Northwords Now:10* and From Glasgow to *Saturn:24.*

Michael Strain is a post-doctoral researcher in the School of Engineering working on nano-photonic devices. He was born and educated in Glasgow and spent time living in Toronto. His work often deals with the strange boundaries between our own experiences and rational knowledge of the world.

Cedric Tai is new to the city and in his first year of the MFA program at the Glasgow School of Art. Coming from Detroit, Michigan, he is slowly adjusting to the abundant dry humor and aggressive friendliness. You can find his artwork on cedrictai.com.

Laura Tansley recently graduated from the University of Glasgow with a PhD in English Literature. She currently works for Widening Participation at the University, writing short-short stories in her spare time.

Rachel Tennant is a Landscape Architect and photographer with an award winning landscape design practice and a successful photographic business. She has a number of academic and photographic books published, but since 1990 she has written poetry as an accompaniment to travelling associated with her photographic and landscape careers. Her work is always influenced by her physical surroundings, whether urban or rural.

Emma Wilson: I am a Graduating English Literature student who grew up in Carluke, just outside of Glasgow. I was particularly influenced by a recent 20th Century fantasy course. Glasgow provides an exciting paradox for investigating the reaction of an uncompromising urban environment breached by the fantastical.

Sarah Weir: I was born in Leith, Edinburgh in 1992 and brought up in Newcastle upon Tyne from the age of four. My heritage has allowed me to have the best of both worlds in terms of what I class as home, yet it was the regional dialect of 'Geordie Land' that provided inspiration for the genre and direction of this piece. I am currently studying English Literature at the University of Glasgow and I hope that one day I will leave my own literary footprint.